VAMPIRE HERO SAGA

WELCOME BACK TO MY

MAD WORLD

SHANE

VAMPIRE HERO SAGA

Distributed through LULU.com

First printing March 2009
Book Printed in America (via digital printer)

ISBN: 978-0-578-02119-5

ART WORK BY Scott Breitenstein

SHANE

GET READY TO DIVE INTO A NEW VEIW OF THE SUPERNATURAL REALM...MINE. I HOPE YOU ENJOY THE TWISTS AND TURNS I DECIDED TO TAKE. THIS IS THE BEGGINGING NOT THE END.

SHANE

This book is dedicated to all the Vampire book lovers, who can hardly wait to read the next tale of the undead. I hope that my twist on an age old theme pleases all of you and you will follow my undead hero throughout his journey.

SPECIAL THANKS TO AJAY HARNAGE AND PEGI

MEZINGO FOR INSPIRING GREAT PARTS OF THIS BOOK.

FOR MY FAMILY AND FRIENDS, I LOVE YOU.

BLOOD BY DAY

BY

W. SHANE WILSON

A VAMPIRE HERO SAGA

VAMPIRE HERO SAGA

SHANE

TABLE OF CONTENCE

SHANE

VAMPIRE HERO SAGA

The Pacific Northwest nights are cold as hell in January, but I no longer feel it. It has been ten years since the night I was attacked in the parking lot of my condo. I am sitting here on the bench of the park next to the I-5 Bridge in Vancouver Washington, it is sixteen degrees out tonight. The cars on the bridge look like Fireflies, and the night is so wonderful. Alone is the night, I often say that to my friends. They don't get me but who does these days.

My tale started as a hum-drum night club manager in a small but upbeat little club. It was a fun job with lots of girls and a hangover most nights. When I took the job at nineteen I thought this was the greatest job in the world, but I was so wrong. How many three day drunks and one night stand can one guy take?` No, I am not bitching, I am plenty thankful for all the blessing I have. I pay all my bills on time and drive a nice enough car; I get laid every so often, so it is not such a bad life.

One exceptionally dark night when the club was smoking, I stayed late to close up and there was a hottie who wanted to play kissy face, so I played along. I was about 4:30 when I got home and the damn parking area street light was out again. I got out of my stang and wobbled toward the gate, because I was a wee bit polluted. I never made it to the gate.

The strongest hands you could imagine grabbed me and pinned me to the ground. I am no fighter, but drunk or not I know when I am in the soup, so I fought back for everything I was worth. It didn't matter, I couldn't do shit. Did I mention that this joker had the strongest hands ever. That night the life I knew was lost, that night I died for the first time. I am Jazon Wild and this is my story.

CHAPTER 1: TODAY I DIED

Jazon lay face down with a giant on his back, he struggled but to no avail. The attacker had the worst breath ever, like coffee and diarrhea. Jazon twisted and still he could not help himself. He tried to call for help because it was almost morning time in his hood and people would be getting up for work as he usually went to bed. The attacker put their hand over his mouth and he could not scream because he could not even breathe.

"Ya shur aer a fighter boyo, but it'll nay help ye" The voice said behind him.

With a sudden brutal yank Jazon was on his knees and a severe pain came in the back of his shoulder. He guessed he just got stabbed, since he did not hear a gun go off. He was about to black out when the only thing he could see was the sun coming up, then nothing.

"Hey man what the hell happened, what is all this blood on your clothes, you kill somebody or what" Ajay said?

"Huh, what, where the hell am I at" Jazon said?

"Bro, your on my couch, good thing my girl didn't come home with me last night you would have scared her to death man" Ajay said.

"What, last thing I remember I was trying to get into my condo and I was jumped. I think I got stabbed or something" Jazon said in a haze.

The best friend Jazon ever had is Ajay, he was big, black, and had shoulders that looked like he had on shoulder pads all the time even though he didn't. Ajay was a semi-pro football player, built like a brick house, luck for everyone Ajay had a gentle soul, because he was built for destruction. Jazon sat on his couch covered in blood, but there was not a single drop of fresh blood on the couch. Ajay went and got Jazon a bottle of water.

"Drink this, I will go get my gaffe and we will go to your place and see if the fool who jumped you wants to dance with both of us" Ajay said with a smile.

The drive back to Vancouver was not a long one but, since Ajay lived in Portland Oregon, Jazon started to wonder how he got the sixteen miles to his friend's crib covered in blood without the po-po jumping on him. Ajay kept looking at Jazon like maybe they should be going to the ER instead of Jazon's house, but he didn't say it. They arrived at the condo and Jazon red Mustang was sitting there in the spot assigned to him. However, when the guys looked they found Jazon's keys and coat on the ground seven or eight

SHANE

feet away, there was dried blood on the ground and Jazon's coat. They looked around but it was only 6:27AM so most people where still inside getting ready for work. Jazon was really confused now, how did he get to Ajay's house, why would he leave his keys on the ground, and what happened last night?

"Hey Jazon did you get mugged last night" Ms. Magenty asked as she got her morning paper? "Is that the hoodlum who done it son"?

"What, no. This is my best mate Ajay. He brought me home after I got jumped maam" Jazon said.

"Well, he black after all and you know" She said.

"Oh Snap, granny just busted me one, not cool maam, I play Pro football, not mug people" Ajay explained with a grin.

   Jazon took a shower and washed off the dried blood, while Ajay looked around Jazon's car to make sure it was secure. The busy body Ms Magenty called the police on Ajay. The police arrested him and then knocked on Jazon's door. The door opened and Jazon was in a towel looking at the cop with a toothbrush in his mouth, and one eyebrow raised.

"Are you Mr. Wild" the officer asked?

"Yes, can I help you" Jazon answered.

"You neighbor called us and said you were jumped by the man in the police car over there. Can you take a look and identify the man before we take him down" the cop asked?

They walked over to the car and there was Ajay in cuffs, in the back of the police cruiser. Jazon looked at the cops and sighed rather loudly.

"Gentlemen you have in your car at this very moment #99 Ajay Rey the running back sack machine from the Portland Riot football team. And he is my best friend" Jazon explained. "I told all of that to the neighbor this morning and she called in a false report, so take her to jail please"?

"Sorry Mr. Rey, you were great last Saturday, 19 tags right" The cop said trying to save face.

"Yeah, I had a good game guys. Next time could we check with the victim before arresting me because I am a black man" Ajay said with a grin.

"Sorry again sir" The cop said.

"Hey man, I got to jet to practice or it is the bench for me bro" Ajay said to Jazon.

The whole day passed and Jazon slept. He usually gets up to pee or something but not this day. He slept like the dead this time. The dreams Jazon had were of faraway places and people he didn't know. He sat up covered in sweat and was so famished that he could barely wait to get to the kitchen to start eating something. Jazon ate nearly everything in his house and was still so hungry. He had never been so empty as this. When Jazon finally ran out of food, he got dressed and went out for a lunch. Jazon loved to get the New York steak the local waffle house. He just about ran there, but he forced himself to calm down and drive.

He got there and luckily there were few customers in the place at this time of day. He sat down and the waiter came over and took his order, the waiter asked him how he wanted his steak and Jazon who liked medium well done said "Just past raw man".

The cook brought Jazon's order to him and hung around for a minute to make sure that Jazon really wanted a semi-raw steak. Jazon almost went nuts when the cook put the blood soaked steak down on the table. Jazon picked it up and ate it with his fingers, and he drank the blood from the plate which made the cook nauseated to watch. Finally, Jazon felt full. Jazon paid the bill and left. The sun was going toward the horizon nearing sundown, a perfect time to go home and take a nap prior to going to work. The bed felt like an old friend when Jazon laid on it. He was asleep in less than a minute. Jazon had the same stranger filled dreams, with the same unknown faces. Jazon moaned and flopped around in his sleep but never woke up.

The phone rang beside Jazon's head, he picked it up and listened to the voice for a moment and then hung it up. He stumbled out of bed and into the shower. He always set out clothing for work prior to going to bed every day, thus he only had to shower, dress, and leave with little or no hubbub. Jazon go to the club and the bouncer he just hired did not recognize him, so when he tried to go in the thug stopped him.

"Oh very funny, get out of the way" Jazon said in a gruff decaffeinated voice.

"No club crashing jack, get in line and pay like everyone else" The bouncer said all tough.

(Laughter).

Jazon removed his sunglasses and looked at the doorman, the guys stepped back startled. Jazon walked right by him in disgust at his stupidity.

The night passed like all the others had for years, only every pretty girl in the club seemed to want to hang out with him. Jazon never had so many beautiful women push up on him, when there wasn't an up-coming party at his club that they wanted to get on the VIP list for. Jazon literally could have had ten women in one bed if he chose and all at the same time. Jazon was not like that though so he had his red haired bartender bail him out. She came and said he promised his bed to her tonight and the disappointed ladies faded away finally.

"Thanks Jax, I owe you one sugar" Jazon said then kissed her on the lips.

SHANE

"Take me home tonight and make me dance and we are even" Jax said all sexy.

The sun came up and Jax and Jazon were still in the throws of passion. Jazon had never been lovers with her, because they were close friends and he thought it was a bad idea. He was wrong, she was the best lover he had ever know in his life, and she never seemed to tire out, but then neither did he for some reason. It was just so good. Finally, Jax had enough and wanted to nuzzle and sleep, so Jazon held her close and sleep with her until noon. Jax woke him up and she looked scared.

"What's a matter Jax you look like you saw a ghost" Jazon asked?

"You bit me and began to suck on my butt, look" Jax said. She pointed and two small bloody hole on her fit butt.

"Sorry bad dream I guess" Jazon said?

"I don't mind baby, but ask first. The bite is not why I woke you up, you were talking in a language I never heard before and your teeth were long and sharp. You opened you eyes and they were pale powder blue. Jazon your eyes are usually brown. Last night they were almost glowing red, now pale white. I thought you were having a seizure or a stroke baby" Jax said shaking.

Jazon pulled her gently into his arms and ran his hands down her back and firm butt. She felt right in his arms, like no woman ever did. He laid her on her back and loved her so softly that she cried from the sensual pleasure he gave her. She moaned six times and then went limp from exhaustion. Jax fell asleep soon after that. Jazon was pleased with how he had made her feel, but he had to admit to himself he was never a great lover, and here he was turning out a goddess like Jax, who have more offers of sex than a porn star. What was happening with him. The huge hunger was on him again, he looked down at his new lover and the hunger jumped in his chest. He jumped back away from her so fast that he was across the room in a instant. How did I do that? Why do I want to eat my girlfriend, and not in a sexy way. Jazon was freaking out.

"Steak, I need raw meat" Jazon said to himself.

The waiter almost gagged when she watched Jazon eat a fresh blood steak and drink the blood. He never wasted a drop. Plate was so clean that is looked like it came straight from the dishwasher. Jazon paid the bill and left. He felt so strong and alive suddenly. He went back to his condo and planned on helping Jax find her inner woman again, only she was not there, but she did leave a note.

(Dear lover boy, I guess you went out to get something to eat and let me sleep off the loving. I am sad to not get to kiss you goodbye but I have a lunch date with

SHANE

my sister and so I washed my goodies and stole you white tank top which is just long enough to be a sexy mini on me. Wish you could see me, maybe not; I would never have been able to pull myself away from you. I have a confession; I have been crushing on you for two years. If I had known you were a animal in bed I would have made a better effort to get you attention. Damn, I am rambling on so. **I LOVE YOU JAZON. XXX)**

"Damn, I want to see you in my shirt" Jazon said out loud to himself.

VAMPIRE HERO SAGA

SHANE

CHAPTER 2: BAD NEWS

Ajay picked up Jazon and they went to the basketball court to meet some other guys they played ball with on Thursdays. Ajay usually carried their team because he was a monster at sports, not just big but fast as a cat as well. They divided into four man teams and the game was on. Jazon hung back and fed Ajay as usual so he could score. This went on for fifteen minutes until everyone was sweating and out of breath. The played at a professional pace and some other players player pro basketball, so the games were a great workout for everyone. However, this time Jazon was not sweating or tired. So when Ajay fed Jazon under the hoop, he bull slammed the ball. Everyone stopped and looked shocked. Jazon was the shortest and usually lamest player. They like him playing though because he didn't give hard or stupid fouls and he could pass like no other and had a decent jumper shot. However, Jazon was gravity bound, he had NO jumping ability. So, when he dunked the ball from a standing position straight up, it caused some surprise.

"What, I have been working on my legs so I can jump better" Jazon said.

"Works for me baby boy, you're a inside threat now, that makes us harder to guard" Ajay said.

The game went on and Ajay tossed some balls up for Jazon to slam. Jazon also could dribble and cross up like a NBA point guard suddenly, which gave the other team fits. After four hard contested games the guys called it a day. They all shook hands, which they did at the beginning and end of every game as a show of friendship and sportsmanship. When they all left Ajay rounded on Jazon with the look.

"Spill white boy" Ajay asked forcefully.

"What" Jazon answered?

"Don't play with me Jazon, are you juicing man. That stuff will kill ya, and it will shrink up your manhood son" Ajay said concerned?

"No Juice. Remember when I got attacked, well every since then when I eat raw meat, I get strong, and I mean really strong brother" Jazon said with a grin.

"Bullshit" Ajay answered.

Jazon did not answer him. He walked over to Ajay's BMW Z4 and picked it up by the bummer and held it there with only one hand.

"Oh Snap man" Ajay said. "Woe put it down before someone sees you"!

"Well, believe me now" Jazon said?

Ajay walked over and looked at Jazon's hands and arms, he felt his shoulders. He pushed Jazon into his car and they left in a hurry. They drove until almost dark before Ajay spoke finally. He had a haunted look on his face.

"Look man, I know you're not juicing. No way with your current muscle mass you could lift my car with only one hand. Even I would strain to lift my BMW, and I am a big dude. Man do not tell or show anyone else that or you are going to be in some trouble" Ajay said seriously.

"Okay you got it, I will keep it all to myself Ajay" Jazon said

It was well past dark when they got back to Jazon's pad. They parked and were going to go into the condo when a voice spoke from behind them.

"I should have finished ya off, ya'nu" The voice said as Ajay got tossed like a ball over the BMW backwards.

A cold hand gripped Jazon's arm and went to throw him to the ground, but this time when Jazon fought back it was not swept away like last time. Jazon yanked forward and was looking at a man about his size with glowing green eyes. The man went to punch Jazon, but Jazon was Kajukenbo trained, so he countered at lightning speed and swept the man's feet out and dropped him like a brick on his face. The pavement cracked under the impact. The man did not

SHANE

stay down though, hell no. He moved like a well oiled killer, which of-course he was. He came at Jazon from the BMW side, was just about on top of Jazon when a metal baseball bat hit the man in the face, a full on home run swing from Ajay who was pissed off and through all of his muscle into it. The man went down real hard and was dazed a bit. Jazon had him by the throat before Ajay even knew he moved. Ajay's best friend's eyes were glowing like two blue laser lights. More, the man was dangling at the end of his out stretch arm a foot off the ground.

"I would consider your word carefully if you don't want to be killed" Jazon growled!

(Insane laughter)

"Boyo, I aim alreedy dard" The man said. "I geeve op, let us chat mate, you need to nu a wee bit, lad before marnin".

"Hold on to him Jazon, that guy is nuts" Ajay said frightened.

"Ken I eat'em mate before we tark" The man asked?

"NO" Jazon said with a final tone.

The man walked right into Jazon condo without any trouble, Jazon was right on his back, Ajay in the rear away from the dangerous unpredictable foe. They shut the door when they were inside and Ajay hit the lights. The man was a green eyed, red haired mess. His clothing was expensive but torn up, Jazon thought he probably looked the same, but he didn't.

"I am Mark O'day and I am a 346 year old vampire boyo" Mark said.

"Did you bite me, and what does that mean for me if you did" Jazon asked in a low tone.

"Aye, I wee nibble boyo, but I did na geet to finish the job, and you turned instead of dying" Mark explained.

"You're a vampire" Ajay asked?

The vampire moved super fast to catch Ajay off guard, but he bounced off Jazon, who grabbed his throat and slammed him into the floor. O'day was shocked at how fast Jazon was. Far fast than the vampire himself was..

"Did you come here to kill me" Jazon asked?

"Yes, but now that you turned, yer mine, so why don't you and me eat the black fella and leave this place" O'day asked.

"He would give you the shits, and you don't own nothing idiot. If you did or were more powerful than me, both Ajay and I would be dead but your not stronger, are you" Jazon said plainly. "If I kill you do I go back to normal"?

SHANE

"No lad, there is no going beck, your stuck fer the rest of you long life" O'day said honestly.

"Mark, I am going to let you go, if you ever come back around my town again I will stake you out in the sun and leave you, how does that sound" Jazon asked?

"A right fine and proper offer, I will be accepting" mark said, as he rose to leave.

Jazon grabbed his arm and growled with his fangs fully extended.

"Do not go near any of my friends or death with be the least of you worries O'day, I am not a nice man" Jazon snarled.

The Irish vampire ran off into the night. Jazon watched him go with the eyes of the night. Jazon realize he could see perfectly in the dark when his eyes were blue like they were currently. Mark stopped only once to wave and saw Jazon's eyes like fire looking back at him and kept going quickly.

"We have to see Father Sully now" Jazon said.

"Jazon that was crazy, I could not even see that guys move, he just disappeared. All I did see was you left eye twitch, then you were gone as well. You catch that fool and body slammed him into the floor, got right up in his fro, then you read him the law. That was PHAT baby" Ajay said all excited. "Jazon you know me, I am all man, but I am scared here boy. Do think he will come back after you sent him stepping like that"?

"Hell yes, we will see him again" Jazon said calmly.

(Later at the church of Father Sully)

The pounding on the chapel door scared Father Sully. He opened the door to see two of his favorite young men. One had a death grip on a bat, the other looked so angry he could kill, and he was wearing sunglasses in the dark. The Father asked the boys to come in and tell him what had happened. Father Sully thought they must have gotten jumped and young Ajay had to put some person down hard, the truth put the Father's faith to the instant test the moment Jazon removed his glasses.

"Dear lord" Father Sully said.

"Don't loose it Father, you are in no danger; I swear to the Lord our God" Jazon whispered.

The boys explained the entire story to the Father, Mark O'day and all. Jazon told the Father who baptized him as a boy that he had to have blood to live, so far bloody steak was doing the trick, but he came close to eating his lover Jax. The three of them talked all night until the sun came up; then went outside.

"Jazon you're in the sun, my son" Father Sully said?

"Yes, I love the morning sun, very pretty Father" Jazon said.

"NO man, vampires can't be in the sun boy" Ajay said suddenly?

"Boys come back into the church. (They stopped in front of the holy water basin), Hold a minute, let me try a little water on you". The Father said as he tossed holy water on Jazon's hand, then face to no reaction.

"Her let me see that" Jazon said and drank some. Once again nothing happened.

"I am confused Jazon, holy water and sunshine does nothing to you, what about a cross" Father asked him.

"I have my silver cross on even now father Sully, I never take it off, notta , I feel great" Jazon said.

"You are very special my son, you must try to protect the innocent from other vampires and monsters, will you do that" Father Sully asked all scared.

Ajay watched his best-friend with a little apprehension, what is Jazon said no. What if he slowly slipped into dark and was lost to him. What if in the end he had to kill his own brother, the guy who had his back his whole life and would never leave him not even with death as the result of staying. However, he was afraid, and that was a new nasty taste in Ajay's mouth, one he knew was going to be there as long as he lived.

"Yes, Father I will do all I can to protect the weak and track down the evil" Jazon said. "Ajay has to help me though, I need him. He is my strong right arm, the only

SHANE

man to stand up with me all my life. I need you to stand up with me now little brother".

SHANE

VAMPIRE HERO SAGA

SHANE

CHAPTER 3: NEW BLOOD

In the next few days after Jazon and Ajay spoke father Sully with and agreed to protect the community from the nasties of the night, Jazon had to figure out how to eat and stay strong without opening himself up to attacks from O'Day and his lots. Although, Jazon was pretty sure the Mark was a solo act, because he was a coward, therefore who would want to hang out with him. It just so happens that Mark O'Day did have a local mate, one dark handsome fellow Bryan Finney a vampire extraordinaire, who was charming and rich. Finney was a dirt-bag, but a slick one, he stayed in Portland Oregon, ran a night spot and tasted more than a few of the lovely ladies in the city. Bryan never got caught when he killed someone, did I mention he was slick, well he is. No, he is not to be admired, just understood for what he is, forget and your likely the next meal.

Jazon went to the local butcher and guy he grew up with and asked him for blood. It was a scene right out of a sitcom, to funny to be real, only it was real and Pat Marks was not amused.

"Get the hell out of here Jazon, I am too busy for your jokes today" Pat said in a huff.

SHANE

"Who is joking, I will pay you for it Pat, but I want it filtered through silk, which I will provide" Jazon said in earnest.

Jazon decide that he had to make this quick and pungent to make Pat understand the seriousness of his request. Jazon was a blur, when he took the knife out of Pat's powerful grasp and cut his apron off in a blink of an eye. Pat went to jump back, he found that he could not, because his feet were dangling 6 inches of the floor. Jazon was holding him aloft. Pat turned ashy. Jazon sat him on the counter and stepped back.

"Sadly Pat, I was bitten by a vampire, now I need blood to live. Not human blood, mind you, just fresh blood if I can get it. That is where I need your help Pat. I am a vampire man, okay swallow it. I don't want to bite you or anyone else, but I need the blood to be strong enough to fight the scum who will bite and kill you regular people" Jazon said.

"Dude, Wow! Sorry but this is a little nuts man. Jazon you're a blood sucker" Pat asked?

"Yes. Will you help me or not Pat" Asked Jazon as his eyes turned pale blue and glowed?

"If I say no I am dead right" Pat asked

"Please don't make me answer that question Pat" Jazon said earnestly.

Ajay came in and looked at Pat and Jazon talking and knew that Pat was scared to death. Pat was a big dumb redneck, but he was a solid guy in spite of the fact. Pat looked at Ajay for some help, Ajay just looked back. Pat must have thought Ajay was a vampire as well because he seemed to shrink in on himself.

"I am not a vamp dude, just my boy is. He is a good guy though, we went to see Father Sully and he blessed Jazon for the holy work of protecting mankind from monsters and stuff" Ajay said.

Pat looked at Ajay hard, then turned to look hard at Jazon.

"Sully blessed you" Pat asked.

"Yes".

"Okay, pigs, cows, lambs blood, what do you need. I will help you, and no I am not going to tell anyone, they would lock me up or try to kill me and you guys" Pat said.

An hour later Jazon and Ajay were headed to the football stadium in Portland for Ajay's afternoon practice session. Ajay was driving slower than normal and it was getting on Jazon's nerves.

"Dude, step on it gramma, what worried we will wreck and die" Jazon asked?

"Hey JW, maybe you can't off yerself by crashing but I will still be dead baby boy" Ajay said.

"Do you think we can trust Pat" Jazon asked?

"Pat is a solid brother Jazon, he is down, don't sweat it" Ajay said.

The rest of the ride was silent as Jazon was lost in thought about what to do about all of his new bologna in life. A new vampire, but not a traditional one, Jazon wondered if it was God's will that he be spared from being a monster. He was going to make sure that if that was the case, then he could not fail in his task, no matter the cost. Jazon looked at Ajay, his BFF since he was nine, what if some monster grabbed his boy? Jax came suddenly to mind, he was never so comfortable with a woman as he was with her. They seemed to be a perfect match pair, was she going to refuse him when he told her about his little problem?

A cell phone rang and both Ajay and Jazon jumped.

"Well answer it man" Ajay said.

Jazon hit send.

"Hey it is Jazon, whas up" Jazon crooned.

"Hey baby, I am so sorry but I had to go earlier I will make it up to you later I promise" Jax said.

"Baby I really need to talk to you about something important" Jazon said.

"You don't have a disease do you. Oh, God that is it, your dirty" Jax said?

"Silly girl, I am clean as a fresh dish washer glass. That is not it. Hey if any creepy red headed guys come up on you, fade quick they are bad ju-ju baby" Jazon said.

"Come get me Jazon Wild, I want to be with you" Jax said sultry.

"I am with Ajay at ball practice, it will take me a little time to get there, hey where are you right now anyway Jax" Jazon asked?

"Your place" Jax said "the door was open".

Jazon was a blur of movement, Ajay saw him like a reflection as he moved. Jazon was a mile away before Ajay stopped the car. Jazon was half way to his condo before Ajay turned his Z4 around.

Jax was startled when the phone went dead and the next instant it seemed Jazon was standing there, his eyes were glowing, and his teeth were pointed and sharp. Jazon went through the condo like a wisp. He stopped finally in front of Jax. He reached out and picked her upi gently and held her to him. Jax could feel his heart, it beat like a humming birds, super fast. Jazon looked angry and scared at the sametime.

"Spill it Jazon, your about to explode" Jax said while placing her tiny hands on Jazon's face.

Jazon looked at her and wanted to die rather than say the words he must say to her, and perhaps loose her. Jazon was nauseated and starving. He took her hand and went to the fridge and pulled out a raw steak and ate it. He brushed his teeth, Jax just waited and touched him constantly.

"I am a vampire Jax" Jazon said suddenly.

"Oh, I thought it was something serious baby" Jax said with a twisted smile. "I gathered something was up will you when you bit my ass last night and spoke a old language that is dead".

"You're taking this pretty good Jax, I thought you would be tripping and tell me to take a hike" Jazon explained.

Jax dried Jazon face with a towel and ran her hand down his back, she sighed and put her face in his neck and nuzzled him, with her hands sliding into his rear pants pockets. Jax leaned up and kissed Jazon.

"I am with you, no matter what" She said with a smile.

"No matter what, you could be killed when Mark comes looking for me and Ajay. God only knows Jax what the hell is really out there. You better be sure that you really think you can handle all of this stuff" Jazon said excitedly.

Jax placed her mouth over his, so he would shut up. They stood there killing, until Ajay burst in with his bat looking scared to death. He saw Jax and Jazon holding each other. He raised one eyebrow.

"Girl you know my boy it a biter, you sure you want to get up in his grill" Ajay said concerned?

SHANE

"I know he is a vampire Ajay, but he is my Vampire and I think I love him, heck I think I always have" Jax said and looked at Jazon very closely. "Yes, I have loved you since we met at the club".

"No Mark JW" Ajay asked?

"I looked around inside and outside and I did not find anything, but I would bet he or a friend is watching this place. It is likely a bad idea stay here, I certainly can't sleep here with her, they might hurt Jax and that is not acceptable, man" Jazon said gruffly.

"What about the club we could stay there, you have the entire top floor to yourself, beside the owner has wanted you to moving for years. What do you say lover, want to move in together" Jax asked?

Ajay looked at them and realized he was a third wheel so he bailed for practice, he was already late. The coach is going to give him the boot for not being on time. Ajay had the Z4 roaring when he hit the highway. He was talking to himself the whole time, grumbling about how he got his neck in the noose again, every time Jazon and he got together, there was always trouble. Ajay usually caused it and Jazon got him out, so Ajay guessed it was his turn to play back up.

The coach was pissed at Ajay, but Ajay just told him to get over it, bench him or whatever, as long as he got out of his face. The coach was shocked Ajay was

SHANE

never late and always polite now he seemed irked and unapproachable. It seemed to the coaching staff that they were better served by letting it go this time, so they did. Ajay ran over everyone at practice, he was unstoppable, and completely silent.

Hours later when Ajay was home in bed, not that he could sleep however, Ajay was thinking about what he was going to do. He was no match for a vampire or anything else, he was a man, but that is it. What if he runs into something he can handle and Jazon is not there to save him or bail him out? It wa thes question that haunted Ajay all night and all the next morning. The answer would shock Ajay to the bone when it finally came.

CHAPTER FOUR: THE DOLL HOUSE

The next two weeks found Jazon and Jax moving into the clubs loft apartment and Jazon fortified it like the White House. Jazon was determined not to let anyone get him and Jax unaware, when they were at home. Ajay seemed to keep his distance when not helping move boxes and furniture. Jazon could physically move it all by himself but for appearances he thought he better have his big strong boy help him out. Ajay was with Jazon in body but never in spirit anymore. Ajay was scared to death and he had never known fear before, Ajay was a big strong man but this was hard for him to come to grips with.

"Hey Ajay, you ok bro" Jazon asked?

"I'm good" Ajay lied.

(Ajay's phone rang).

"Hey you got Ajay" Ajay answered.

The look on Ajay's face was not one that would lead you to believe that the conversation was a pleasant one that was to Ajay's liking. It would seem the exact opposite. For a black man Ajay was awful green suddenly, like he was going to puke. Then the caller hung up. Ajay closed his phone and settled himself and looked hard at Jazon.

SHANE

"Time to keep our promise to Father Sully boy" Ajay said.

"What we got" Jazon asked?

"Hey I am coming too" Jax said

"NO" yelled Ajay and Jazon in unison.

"Why not" Jax asked?

"This is not a game, we are dealing with killers Jax and if they got you, I would never be able to forgive or live with myself, I think I love you lil' girl and I will not risk your life" Jazon said swiftly.

"No, only mine" Ajay muttered.

Jazon looked at him sideways, but did not comment.

The Doll House was a whorehouse in the south Portland area, it took Ajay an hour to find it even with his GPS. When they finally found it they knew it right away, because Jazon's eyes went red. Ajay noticed and shuddered.

"What does red eyes mean man" Ajay asked, "I know what light blue means, you're pissed and ready to kill"?

"There are supernatural creatures here, maybe vampires, I am not sure though, but more than human Ajay, so I want you to put on a cross and take this silver dagger I bought for you. If you get threaten Little brother, kill without hesitation and do it hard and fast, or you will be dead" Jazon said as he got out.

The two would be heroes went into the pleasure palace, not for fun, but to kill the evil inside. They were greeted at the door by an ugly troll of a man. He looked them over, then stepped aside letting them enter.

"Normal human, but dangerous because he knows what is in here, he smells like monster sex" Jazon said.

"Damn man, you can tell all that by looking at him" Ajay asked?

"No, I can smell it on him, and it is not a pleasant smell bro, be happy you don't have my sense of smell, you would hurl" Jazon chuckled.

"Damn" Ajay whispered, then he hit the doorman with a snapped elbow shot to the chin.

(Jazon smile)

There was music coming from the hallway up in front of them, it was new, on the radio often enough to recognize it. There was also low husky voices that sounded like they were about to engage in sex, or already were. Jazon looked at Ajay and made a; be quiet sign. Ajay shook his head that he got it. Jazon looked carefully into the door. There were two vampire girls sucking a fat man in his mid-fifties on both sides of his neck. The fool did not even know he was about to die. Jazon made a hand sign that there were two long tooth types in the room and where they were in the room according to a clock model. Ajay pulled his dagger out and got ready.

The girls looked up; they had blood covering their gorgeous breasts and naked bodies. The sight of them was not enough to even pause; Ajay or Jazon who stormed into the room. The first girl went to move away from Ajay's dagger but Jazon caught her and threw her at Ajay who stabbed her while she was airborne, took her to the ground and kept stabbing her in the chest. The other one was faster and much smarter; she tried for the window only to find a demon eyed Jazon staring her down from the window. She lost her head in one flit of a move by Jazon's left hand. Jazon took a deep breath and ripped her ribs apart; he tore her heart out and toss it into the fire place, then her head as well.

"Man, this is nasty work bro" Ajay said as he stood up.

Like lightning the vampire Ajay thought he had killed moved to bite Ajay's calf.

"Damn" Ajay said.

Jazon stomped her head flat and then took Ajay's hand, the one with the dagger and cut her head off and tossed it into the fire, her heart followed.

"Heads and hearts Ajay, both have to be removed from the body if you want to kill them permanently, or they will get up and kill you instead" Jazon said flatly as his blue eyes blazed in the fire light. Oh, shit we are in for it now"!

"What is it man" Ajay asked.

Jazon did not answer, his blue eyes turned white and he moved Ajay behind him as the wall exploded into the room. There was six of them, all hyped up with blood dripping from their mouths and there blue eyes shining like a high rocker star.

"Fresh meat, yum" A blood sucker said.

The last words of an over confident vampire, Jazon took his head off with a left sweeping move and punched his heart out through his back with his right hand. The other fire jumped back.

"Better be sure" Jazon warned!

"Who are you, why are you here? This is our hideout and trap for humans, and you just killed two valuable vampire girls; now who is going to get these cattle to come in here and let us drink them" A blond vampire asked?

"Well now isn't that just too bad for you" Jazon said.

All hell broke loose as the remaining five vampires lost their tempers and rushed Jazon and Ajay.

"Oh shit" Ajay said as he stabbed a vampire from under Jazon's extended arm in the heart, then slit his throat fast.

Jazon grabbed Ajay by the arm and threw him at the window. Ajay hurdled through and sun light came streaming through. Ajay was on the ground bitching but alive that was all Jazon needed. Ajay was out of the way and alive.

"Your time has come boys" Jazon said as his pure white eyes had red streaks running through them.

Ajay knew Jazon was hosed and he got tossed out window to save his life. Well, Ajay was not about to let Jazon die in that hell hole alone. Ajay used his strong arms and back to tear down the fracture wall down. There was a sudden Golden brown blur and the outer wall gone to splinters. Before Jay was a 7' werewolf, it never looked at Jazon. It faced the five blood suckers and snarled.

(ROAR)!

"How dare you show your face here mongrel" the blond vampire yelled?

Jazon looked at the werewolf and it just pointed at Jazon's enemies. The gesture was clear enough; the wolf was there for them and was at least for now on Jazon's side. Ajay came through the fractured open wall with his metal baseball bat in hand. The wolf never looked at him either; it just gave a sniff and a nod, and then attacked the vampires.

SHANE

"Watch you ass AJ" Jazon yelled as he also attacked.

The blond vampire was the last to die, and he went down hard. The second to last to die was a smelly black haired nightmare. It attacked Ajay when the wolf and Jazon were busy with the other four vampires. Ajay saw the black haired one lunge at him, he swung his bat as hard as he could, it connected on the vampire's nose. The vampire was sent careening into the fire place, it got up and came at Ajay again this time low like a snake. Ajay did not take the bait, he pulled the dagger Jazon gave him and slammed into the back of the vampire's neck; pinning his head for a second to the floor. Ajay stepped on the monsters back and gave his head a full golf swing strike with his bat. The result was the head came off. The body did not die though; it bucked Ajay off his back and grabbed his ankle.

"OH SHIT" Ajay said!

Te vampire's headless body jumped up and started to drag Ajay across the floor toward his head. Ajay grabbed the dagger out of the floor and cut the Achilles tendon on the vampire's right ankle; that caused it to topple over. Ajay was up and on the torso in a lightning fast moved, he plunged the dagger into the vampire heart and ripped the ribs out of his ay with his powerful hands, Ajay reach in and tore the black heart out and hurled it into the fire place. Ajay walked

SHANE

over to the head and scowling he soccer kicked it into the fire as well.

"Peace ya blood sucking freak" Ajay said as he jumped down out of the house into the parking lot and the sun.

I was thirty-three minutes later that Jazon and the wolf came out of the three story house and set it a blaze. The wolf walked over and placed and huge hand on Ajay's shoulder painfully slow and gave a power squeeze. Ajay was for some reason not afraid and let it happen. The Werewolf looked at Jazon with it's curious black gold rimmed eyes and then it bowed a little and burst to speed toward the under brush. It was gone in that instant.

"Not to bitch little brother but we need to get on out here now, before the poe-poe show" Ajay said.

"Right" Jazon said as they got in the car and left.

They drove in silence all the way back to the club. Ajay looked like he was about to cry and then he did. He stopped the car and cried without shame for a long time. Jazon said nothing. Jazon was in awe of his mortal friend; Ajay beat a vampire male, and not a young one, all by himself and lived to tell the story. Ajay was one seriously brave man.

"Man...I thought I was going to die" Ajay manage to gargle out. "I have never so scared to death before. I am brave, or I thought I was"?

(Chuckle).

SHANE

Ajay looked at Jazon in surprise, because he was pouring his heart out and his best friend; who was more like a brother was laughing at him. Jazon stopped and looked at Ajay hard.

"I tossed you out the window to save your life and what do you do, grab a bat and come back in. You are the brave man I know Ajay, no shit. I was scared I was going to get you killed" Jazon told his friend.

"I would rather die a thousand deaths than leave your back unprotected and alone. I had to come back in, I won't ever leave you to face this alone, not ever" Ajay said tears still in his eyes!

"I know, that is why I think you're the bravest man I know. Despite you fear, you act with bravery and valor; even though you know it might cost you your life. I will never let it come to that. A day may come the I have to go it alone, don't fight me on it Ajay, if I die that is one thing, but you never asked for any of this, and it is shitty of me to drag you into it" Jazon said his eyes a fiery blue flame.

"The only way I won't get your back is if I am already dead, little brother and I will fight you on that" Ajay said.

For the first time in a since Ajay had found out that Jazon was undead, Ajay was actually with his boy all in, no hesitation at all. Fighting for his life and seeing Jazon's life hang in the balance, made Ajay see again the only thing that changed between him and Jazon was Ajay's attitude. So it had all come to a head and Ajay realized he was the problem; the thing bothering Ajay was Jazon was the strongest one now and Ajay felt less of a man. But Jazon saw Ajay as his strong right arm as always, Ajay was going to play that role as well as he could as long as he could, as long as he lived.

SHANE

CHAPTER 5: THE TRUTH

Jax woke Jazon up by kissing him and the lips, no matter how hungry Jazon got Jax blood smelled to him like love not food, so he never bit her again. Kissing however was just what he wanted from her everyday for the rest of his life. A sad thought came to him just then. He was going to live to be very old and she was not. He wanted to turn her but what if she turned into one of them; he could not take it if he had to kill his beautiful red haired lover. Jax knew his face so well that she could nearly read his mind.

"What is the matter lover" Jax asked as she slipped her body on top of his?

"I don't want to live forever without you, but I am scared shitless if I bite you, you will become evil like Mark O'day" Jazon told her.

Jax muscular leg slid softly up and down Jazon's and he mouth kissed his chest, and then his mouth.

"Let's make love not worry about the future" Jax said as she began to do just that.

The lean hips and butt of Jax were doing a very good impression or gentle wave rolling in and out as she pleasured herself and Jazon at the same time. Jazon like it when Jax made love to him from the top,

SHANE

she made the cutest faces as her efforts increased and her pleasure built, not to mention Jax was an excellent lover. Jazon's mouth found Jax's FIRM breast and began to help her find her inner woman. Jax exploded in a rush of pleasure and lay on Jazon's chest and panted. Jazon rolled his tiny lover on to her back and they began again, less vigorously though because Jazon did not want to break her by accident, he could be pretty aggressive sexually with Jax, but since he loved her he was always damn careful with her, Jax knew this and it made their bond diamond solid. Not to mention she loved Jazon more than her next breath.

"Round two baby" Jazon said?

"Give it to me bad-boy" Jax said teasingly.

(Giggles).

Jazon nibbled on her neck as their belly buttons slid back and forth, he would kiss her passionately but her breath was always raspy with effort not to cum to fast, Jazon was a good lover, but when it came to Jax, he was fantastic for her. They had perfect physical chemistry; and every other kind of chemistry as well. Their universe started and stop with each other. Jax was about to loose it again and Jazon pulled away from her and flipped her like a pancake on to her to her belly. Jazon's power hands were on her tiny hips and she leaned back into him. Jazon made Jax moan and purr like a tiger until she came again, and then he came as well.

SHANE

"Wow, that was great" Jazon said stretching his back.

"UMMMMMHHH" Jax said with her face still buried in a pillow.

Jazon lifted his trim lover and cradled her in his arms. Jax put her left hand on the back of his neck, her face on his shoulder and opened her green eyes to look deep into his eyes.

"I love you Jazon, and I could do this everyday all day for the rest of my life" Jax said.

"That is what I am talking about, but I am starving Jax. We need to both eat and renew our strength for round three and four" Jazon said with a laugh.

(Later after a good breakfast at the waffle house).

Jazon was leaving the Building where he loved to eat at; he saw out of the corner of his eye a strange deformed guy running up an alley. Jazon burst to speed, which as far as he knew was the greatest speed any living or undead creature match and live. Jazon did not know how fast he was compared to most vampires, but so far he was faster than all of the ones he ever met. Jazon made it into the alley just in time to see the deformed one going into a door in the wall hidden behind a dumpster. Jazon took two steps and burst through the door literally. Pieces of door flew all over the place.

"What in the name of God" Jazon asked out-loud.

Jazon was attacked by creatures he did not even know the names of. Jazon was faster and stronger than they were but there were a lot of them, the place was jammed with creatures of every kind. Jazon knocked them flying off him and screamed.

"STOP IT" Yelled Jazon.

Everyone stopped moving for a moment and then moved to renew their attacks when Jazon's eyes turned white, and his cross fell out of his freshly torn shirt.

"Wait, stop please" A husky voice said.

All the creatures froze waiting in place. Jazon looked around for the voice and was startled when there came a tug on his left pant leg.

"Woe" Jazon jumped back.

There standing; was a tiny plump fellow with a pointy green hat and long black beard with silver flicks. He was looking at Jazon with expert eyes. This small man had a persona that spoke of wisdom and knowledge. The tiny guys walked up closer to Jazon and the monsters growled cautiously; He waved them off.

"What are you" The tiny plump fellow asked?

"What am I? What the hell kind of question is that? I am a man" Jazon asked?

"Yes, Yes, but what kind of man" the tiny man asked?

Jazon did not know whether to be offended or amused. So he smiled as he chose amused.

"I am Jazon Wild, I am a good man. I am also unique. You see, I was bitten by a vampire but never turned; well I did not become one of them. I am immune to garlic, sunshine, holy water, crosses and so forth. Other vampires are my enemies" Jazon explained.

There was a general buzz after Jazon's speech until the little man stopped it by clapping his hands.

"I don't believe you" The little man said.

"What don't you believe" Jazon asked?

"If you're a vampire, then you can not be immune to crosses and so on, it is God's law son" the tiny guys said.

Jazon pulled out his cross and showed his fangs, and then let his eyes go from brown, to red, to blue and then to pure white.

"I don't eat people; I get my blood from a butcher shop Pat Marks runs on 3rd street. Father Mick Sully is my spotter, a couple of nights ago; me and Ajay cleaned out the Doll House and burnt the mother down" Jazon said with a chuckle.

"That was you" the tiny guy ask?

"Yes" Jazon answered.

The room changed and there were many mutters and side conversation in many languages. This time the little man did not stop the conversations. He reached out and grabbed Jazon's hand with his tiny one and shook it.

"I am Tad Oreilly; I am a gnome. I am six hundred years old and I generally speak for them" Tad said as his hand swept the warehouse.

"Why are you people hiding in here" Jazon asked?

"Oh dear boy you have so much to learn if you are to survive" Tad explained.

The creature in the corner; which was huge stayed away from Jazon, it looked like it was shaking in fear, hell most of them were. Tad led Jazon to a table with different sized chairs and the gnome sat down.

"Let me start by saying I feel no evil in you, which scares me lad. Any who, the world you know is different from the one we know. Vampires rule the world, and the strongest ones whole countries, and they all have clan ties. We are their food source and slaves. Humans are not widely kill and drank, it would attract too much attention, so we are the preferred source of blood. Werewolves are the daylight guardians of the vampires, but that is only because the blood drinkers hold a loved one as hostage to keep them in line. If the hold was ever broken the final war would begin" Tad explained.

Everyone was silently watching Jazon. His reaction stunned many and confused the rest.

Jazon was pissed off, his face was red and his eyes were a rolling thunder of white, it honestly looked like white moving clouds in his eyes.

"You have just inherited a friend and protector. I believe I was given the boons I was to take down all of my cousins, your enemy is now my enemy Tad and all of you" Jazon said in a serious tone.

"Would you really risk your life for us" Said a soft little voice.

Jazon turned and saw a girl who had brown wood colored hair and brown-red eyes, and a deep tan body, she was nearly nude, and her body was wrapped in a sheer green scarf.

"Silky" Tad explained.

"Nice to meet you" Jazon said holding out his hand.

Silky dance forward and shook his hand. Her skin was like super smooth leather, soft but durable. When Silky touched Jazon's hand she smiled, it was like the sun coming out; and she lean forward and put her arms around him and hugged him close. Silky smelled like fresh spring rain over a flower garden. There were a few grumbles when Jazon hugged Silky, she pulled back and spoke.

"He is in love" Silky said!

(Cheers).

"What the hell is that about" Jazon asked Silky?

Silky turned her attention to Jazon and spoke soft.

"Evil does not know love; they can't understand sacrifice or compromise. You are in love with a red hair woman, so you are to be trusted and cared for and about, my new brother" Silky said

Silky kissed Jazon and not in a sisterly way, it made him hot instantly. She really was silky and not just her name.

Ajay came looking for Jazon with his metal bat in his strong right arm. Ajay had a sixth sense about Jazon; he always seemed to be able to find him where ever he was. So hide and seek sucked for Jazon as a kid when Ajay was it, LOL.

"Where did you go boy, and why is the hair on my neck sticking up" Ajay asked himself.

Ajay walk up the alley and looked behind the dumpster. There was a door way there with a board over it, so Ajay shoved the dumpster back and pushed the board out of the way. A werewolf dove on Ajay as her entered the room. They flew sideways and before they hit the floor Ajay was right side up and bringing

SHANE

the bat down hard on the Wolf's head. A strange thing happened; a hand caught the bat just before it smashed the head in. Ajay was startled when he saw the hand belonged to Jazon. Ajay had swung as hard as he could and Jazon just stopped it as if it was just hanging out there limp. Ajay killed a vampire recently and it would have been flattened by that blow but Jazon was not even fazed. How much stronger was Jazon over average?

"Hey brother Ajay; would you mind not busting this dudes head? We are no longer alone" Jazon said as his hand swept the room.

"Damn, this place is full of monsters" Ajay said.

"Piss off asshole" Said a three eyed giant.

Ajay looked at him and showed him the bat, to make sure he did not misunderstand Ajay. Keep clear, that was the message. Silky did not read the message; she walked up and put her tan arms around Ajay. She did not smile.

"You are scared, and your heart is troubled, you believe that either you are going to watch you brother die or loose your own life in the conflicts to come. You must not fear ebony one, you have an inner strength that will carry you through. You only have to believe it, and in yourself and him" Silky said pointing at Jazon.

"You...baby you smell great" Ajay said with a grin.

SHANE

Silky kissed him on the lips, he dropped the bat and swooped her up into his powerful arms and they kissed for awhile. When Ajay finally put the wood nymph down, Jazon was in deep conversation. The was a man, a boy with soft green eyes and a tiny person and the giant werewolf transformed back to a man, a black man named Enoch. Ajay walked over and looked at him and sat down, Silky sat on Ajay's lap.

"I think we need to kill the Prince of Portland, he likely is the keep of that lil bastard mark O'day" Tad said gruffly.

"He is well protected, so if you want to kill him you better be ready to die to do it" The man at the table said. He turned and looked at Ajay. "Hey I am Wolf Peters, nice to meet you".

The man reached out and nudged Silky and then shook hands with Ajay. Ajay thought something about him was familiar, but he could not grasp it...yet.

"Anyway, back to Finney; I want him dead as much as he wants me dead, but I can't get close to him without killing my brothers" Wolf said.

"Who is Finney? If someone wants to kill you then kill them back, me and Jazon had to do that in a whore house, simple really" Ajay said.

"Not simple, they are my siblings, my own blood, and they can't help themselves. They do not deserve to die for that. Finney is Brian Finney vampire lord over all of

Portland Oregon. You have no idea how big this joker is son. Brian has the entire crime world on the west coast in his pocket, human and non-human. To kill that bastard will take a miracle" Wolf said.

"Okay, but still look at you guys all strong and able, why not start breaking down his organization little by little, weaken him until you can get close enough to kill him" Ajay said.

"You are so young and naïve. Finney can't be taken that way, if we break down an area of his operation, he will kill his own people for letting it happen, he cares nothing for anyone but himself, we have to strike all at once or leave here for good and let Finney have this coastline to do as he wishes" Enoch said.

Ajay looked around the table and realized other than the boy and Wolf he was likely the only humans in this place, so he felt if he could man up so could they.

"Look, I am scared shitless most of the time now, but I am not going to puss out and leave the job to someone else, you say your at war than act like it, kick this fool in the nuts and let him know your after him, dog him until he wants you so bad he get reckless and then we pop him" Ajay said. "Or you can hide in the dark like a little kid and cry in your cereal"!

(ROAR).

SHANE

Enoch and several other lunged at Ajay all at once, they never even got close, Jazon flattened all of them with palm strikes to the gut. No one was hurt, but they all were winded from the blows. Tad whistled, he had never seen such speed before. He was old and powerful, he was a magic user, this unlike duo; one vampire and one human may be just what it takes to put Finney on his back for good.

"There will be no fighting, you want to fight go find Finney or one of his crew and fight them" Jazon said! "Ajay my brother, stop pushing these people, they have been facing this horror for centuries and we have only just begun, patience and understand please. We must all work together to survive, therefore we can't fight each other ever".

"Sorry man" Ajay said. "I just can't sleep anymore, I close my eyes but I always see death, mine, yours, everyone's, I would rather fight and go down; than live on my knees even for a second".

Tad looked at Ajay and knew Jazon had a good man at his back, one who would not hesitate even to save his own life, when the time to act came. Wolf seemed to think the same thing. Wolf was not one to give loyalty or friendship easily, and he appeared to like and respect both of these men already.

"We...I would like to ask a favor. We need food and supplies and most of us don't look human enough to shop or move around during the day, can you arrange for our needs Boys if we pay you" Wolf asked?

Both Ajay and Jazon smiled and at Wolf and then at each other.

"You can pay for the food and supplies, but we are not for hire" Jazon said.

(Shocked faces and disappointment).

"Very well, we will find another way" Wolf said.

"I knew they would not help us" Cried a tiny winged creature.

Jazon moved so fast that the wings creature was in his arms before anyone could blink. Jazon walked softly back to the table cradling the tiny creature in his powerful grasp.

"You misunderstand us. We will not take you money, but that is because we are your friends, our help is not something you have buy, it is freely given and always will be from here on or until we are dead" Jazon explained.

"That's right, we are a team, we need each other to win this war, so I will do everything I can to help you" Ajay said.

The tiny creature giggled as Jazon rubbed her neck gently. Wolf smile and so did Tad. Most of the other creatures were relived and jovial at this development.

SHANE

"Are any of you God fearing beings" Jazon asked?

"We are all God fear creatures; it is only our faith in God that has carried us through all of these years" Tad said.

Both Ajay and Jazon smiled big time.

"We have an idea of how to help your people can get what they need continually and not attack attention to yourselves. Father Sully will be pleased and he will want to provide you with Bibles and prayer support as well as physical" Jazon explained.

"What do you have in mind lads" Tad asked/

"We order your supplies and have it delivered to the church or community center, they get big deliveries all the time, a few more will not be noticed and you can pick them up in the dead of the night under Father Sully's protection and ours" Ajay said.

"Brilliant" Silky said.

The little wood nymph pulled Ajay aside and spoke softly so only he could hear.

"Can I go home with you, I can sense when an enemy approaches and I can tell if a person is lying, so you can never betaken unaware. I also like you and would lay with you in comfort, you please my senses ebony man" Silky said.

"Girl are you for real, you are so fine, you came come by my crib anytime" Ajay said softly.

SHANE

(Later at the church).

"I have a surprise for you and a challenge Father Sully" Jazon said.

"Please call me Mick; since we are in cahoots these days on bigger issues than my name Jazon" Father Sully said.

"Mick I have a mission that only you can do, it can be dangerous, but likely will not be, are you interested" Jazon asked?

The wily preacher knew when he was being set up for something, and this was definitely one of those times. Still Jazon was a friend and a gift from God so he would play along.

"Speak your piece Jazon, I will consider what you ask before I commit to it" Mick said with a grin.

Jazon explained everything for the next half hour, he left out the foul language and the parts where they attacked each other. However, he put in that although these were not humans, they were all God's children and they need a Shepard and help that the pastor could provide. The look on Father Sully's face was priceless. He looked afraid and then he looked angry. Finally he smiled and regarded Jazon.

SHANE

"I knew you were going to be my big test or my life's work when you and Ajay were boys, but I had no idea how much of a test you would both become. I may not be up to the challenge, but it will not go untested because I am unwilling to try. I have faith that God will show me the way Jazon, so YES, I will help your new friends with whatever I am able to provide" Mick said with a grin.

Wolf and Tad stepped out of a shadow that Mick Sully did not know was even there, Enoch was right behind them.

"You were right he is a good man, he has true faith in God so he is willing to take it on that faith that we are his responsibility. We are happy to make you acquaintance" Tad said as he held out a tiny hand to shake.

Father Sully smiled and shook his hand. He shook Wolf's and Enoch's as well. Then he turned and looked serious at Enoch.

"You are not a human, are you? May I see your true self" Father Sully asked?

Enoch took two steps back and shifted into full werewolf mode. Werewolves shift, change is the wrong word. If you ever see a man turn into a werewolf it looks like a bullet being chamber and then fired. You know cocked, locked and ready to rock. To Mick Sully's credit he did not even move when Enoch

SHANE

walked up and looked down at him from far above. Enoch was now at the least eight feet and five hundred pounds. Mick reached out and felt the fur on Enoch's stomach; and then he smiled.

"Truly magnificent; I have never seen anything that compares to the wonder you just showed me. Thank you Enoch for showing me this person thing, that was very generous of you. Now down to business gentlemen, do you have a shopping list for me" Mick asked?

"Yes we do and we have the money for all that we want to order" Tad added promptly.

"Look my fine fellow, I will never question your honesty or motives as long as you don't force me too. You and I will do the accounting together, to ensure your needs are met and it all balances, because this can not go on the books, so we will have a private ledger" Mick explained.

"I believe we are going to get on quite well Father Sully. Now, I would like you to come and provide us with a proper service for worshipping God, are you willing" Tad asked?

(Gut busting laughter).

SHANE

"Oh my God Tad; I would be a sorry servant of the lord if I did not want to jump this opportunity to help bring the word of God to your extended family. Yes I would be greatly honored to speak the lord's words for you and yours" Father Sully said.

Wolf turned and watched Jazon, watching the strange boy that the seemed to be Wolf's shadow. Wolf was instantly nervous and apprehensive. Wolf did not know the Jazon was aware he was watching him.

"What is the boy's name" Jazon asked startling Wolf?

"Biz" Wolf answered in haste and wished he had not.

"Biz that is a unique name" Jazon said.

Wolf almost jumped back when Jazon looked at him his eyes were crimson, but there was no malice in his face.

"Yes my eyes are red; that means that there is more to you and Biz than meets the eye Wolf. My eyes tend to turn red around non-humans and such, so care to tell me your stories man" Jazon explained?

"Maybe later Jazon" Wolf said.

Wolf hoped Jazon would drop the subject, however he knew that even if he did this conversation was not over by a long shot. Wolf was not necessarily afraid of Jazon but he was not idiot, Jazon was fast and stronger and deadly. It was only this unusual man's good heart and strong mind that made him safe to be

SHANE

around. Wolf hoped the day would never come when he had to oppose this man, for that day would surely be Wolf's last.

"He guys I gotta blow, Ajay and I are taking Jax and Silky out for dinner, so I better get a move on" Jazon said as he went to get into his Mustang.

"What, are you trying to get her killed" Enoch roared.

Jazon turned on Enoch and his eyes were white with fire dancing in them as if he expected to be attacked. Enoch reel at the dead gaze and stepped back, hell they all did, even the pastor.

"Enoch, have you ever really looked at Silky, she has an exotic look, but there is nothing about her to say she is not human, she is quite safe with Ajay and me for dinner, and if you don't start being less abrasive I might have to smack you on the noise with a news paper" Jazon said.

There was a moment of terse silence and then riotous laughter. Enoch did not catch on right away; he just looked at the rest of the guys laughing perplexed. Sudden ly he got it. You hit a dog on the noise with the paper so he can get paper trained for your house. It was a joke, because he was a wolf. It was very funny Enoch realized and he laughed as well.

(Later at dinner).

SHANE

Jax dressed her and Silky alike, which was easy since they were the same size. Silky was dress in a short light green mini dress that showed of her hard pert breasts and perfect legs. Jax was in her little red man killer mini dress that was open across her breast, stomach and back. You could not wear this dress unless you were very fit, because the dress covered only the bare essentials nothing more. The girls had both Jazon and Ajay drooling like idiots, which is just what Jax had in mind. Both Ajay and Jazon were dressed nice in silk shirts and black slacks. Both men wore crosses around their necks. The restaurant staff were wowed by the group, first Ajay was a pro ball player, Jazon was a local club manager and part owner and he was good looking and friendly, but the ladies were breath taking and smelled so good that it made you swoon if you inhaled around them. It was Silky, she released a pheromone into the air that made everyone amorous.

"Let's order" Ajay said.

Silky ordered a salad because she was a wood nymph and did not eat meat. Ajay and Jax order New York steaks well done with a baked potato. Jazon told the waiter to bring him a raw rib-eye steak, with only seasoning on it. The waiter looked agast.

"Sir that is not good for you" The waiter said.

(Four people laughed out loud).

"Look friend, I would ask for a cup of blood but I think it would scare the rest of the patrons. So please bring me a blood fresh uncooked steak and don't argue" Jazon said.

"Yes sir" The waiter said!

The staff watched as Jazon and his company ate like hungry bears and then went into the ballroom and danced the night away. Little did any of them know that Brian Finney himself was watching them with an expert eye.

VAMPIRE HERO SAGA

SHANE

CHAPTER 6: THE SWAMP

Life for Ajay was P.H.A.T, his best friend was the toughest MO in town, his girl was a supernatural beauty and he was alive to enjoy his life; all in all, a good time. All that was about to change for the worse. Father Sully called Ajay and told him to come to the church immediately. Ajay had Silky sleeping on his chest and he did not want to let her go just now; however Mick's voice was troubled. Ajay woke up his baby and kissed her goodbye.

When Jazon arrived at the church Ajay was there with his bat in his hand and a snub-nosed shotgun was slung across the back of his shoulders. Ajay also had the deadly dagger blessed by the Father in a new leather sheath on his belt. Ajay's face was grim.

"What happened now, you look so down in the mouth" Jazon asked?

Wolf answered for Ajay and the assemble group standing just outside of the south entrance of the church.

"A few days ago two girls were reported missing. They were found this morning floating in the marsh area south west of Eugene, dead and drained of blood" Wolf explained.

Jazon looked irritated and he closed his eyes and pondered the news for a moment. When he opened his eyes, he spoke in direct orders.

"Ajay and I are going to go down there and kill what ever is responsible for the deaths. I need Enoch and Biz to keep and eye on our girls while we are gone. I want Father Sully to bless me and Ajay and everything we take with us, so we have as much good karma and love as we can carry" Jazon explained.

No one argued, Jazon was a natural leader and he thought before he spoke. If there was any trouble Jazon was the first one in and the last one out. Father Sully went right to work blessing Ajay and Jazon's gear and then the young men themselves. Biz who never spoke touched Ajay on the arm and nodded and then ran over to Ajay's Z4 and drove it baby to Ajay's place to stay with Silky until Ajay came back. Biz, Wolf and Ajay seemed to be carrying on a secret comradeship that Jazon was not aware of.

Enoch was not happy about staying behind until he arrived at the club and met Jax and the other hot girls that worked there. Enoch changed his tune and was more than happy to do his part. Jax who had talked on the phone with Jazon knew Enoch was a werewolf and she reminded him of why he was there, still it was nice to have a big strong mean looking black man around to keep the drunks from trying to rape her staff.

Silky was close to Biz, like twins close, Silky had adopted Biz as a little child and they grew up together. He almost never spoke; that bothered everyone except Silky and Wolf, who knew why the young man never spoke. Silky wanted to go protect her man, but was happy the Biz was with her while Ajay was gone hunting.

(In the mustang on I-5 headed south)

"Man, I ain't no Cajun to be going into a swamp and liking it. I am a city boy; not to mention the coach was pissed I am missing a weeks practice before a semi final game. I am so far in the dog house right now I don't think I will ever get out" Ajay said.

"Well if you want to go back I guess I can take care of this alone" Jazon said.

Ajay turned and looked at Jazon with an incredulous face. However, Ajay stopped belly aching after that.

Hours later when they found the place that Father Sully sent them to; It was a small boat launch area in the weeds literally. Jazon got out, popped the trunk, took out his swords and his box of sharpened pencils which he put in his pocket. Ajay had his dagger already, but he took the shotgun out and slung it over his shoulder; he took his trust bat out and closed the trunk.

SHANE

"Guess we might as well get this show moving huh"
Ajay said.

"Yeah, guess so" Jazon replied.

They walked down the boat launch and noticed
there was a small flat boat tethered to the bank. Jazon
pointed at the boat. They inspected it, it was complete
and in good shape so they took it out into the wet
lands and began to search for the killer of the girls.

The sky was getting dark and the air was cold but
Jazon did not seem to know it. But then again he was a
vampire and could see in the dark as if it were high
noon. The cold actually bothers vampires, they can
ignore it but they get cold just like normal humans do.
Apparently not all vampires are cold blooded, so are
warm blooded, Jazon was one of those. So when Ajay
said it was cold, Jazon agreed. Jazon spoke very softly
as not to make any sound at all.

"There is a house and a small fire off to our right about
five hundred yards, let's head for that" Jazon said.

"Sounds good" Ajay said with caution.

They rowed quietly to a small island miles from
anywhere. It was perfectly hidden from the air and
surrounding area by odd overgrowth of trees and
reeds. If Jazon and Ajay would had been here during
the day they might just passed it by. However, at night
with a fire burning it stood out like a lighthouse in a
storm. Find a place to land was no easy chore. Jazon's

sharp vampire eyes found a small private landing expertly hidden in the overgrowth. Jazon did not have to tell Ajay that he believed they should be careful. Ajay was more alert and ready that Jazon had even seen him be before. Once again Jazon regretted risking Ajay's life.

"You lead Little brother, your eyes are better than mine in the dark" Ajay whispered.

They weary explorers approached the fire slowly, but not slow enough because they were met by a hail of buck shot.

(Kaboom).

Both young men hit the deck and scrambled behind the small trees. Ajay whipped his gun off his shoulder and was about to fire back when Jazon waved him off. Another blast nearly changed his mind. One of the bullets found Jazon's forearm. Jazon snapped open his Buck knife and dug the bullet out of his arm. I burned un-naturally, in his palm. Jazon decided to put it in his pocket for later review. In a flash Jazon was on his feet and moving at a rate of speed even in broad daylight would have made him seem invisible. The person shooting at Ajay's position was a medium built little old lady, but tall.

SHANE

"Hey, what gives" The lady said as Jazon ripped the shotgun out of her hands.

"Hey yourself grandma" Jazon said in a huff.

A head popped up in the trees and then down again stealthy.

"Is it ok to come out, I am not going to get blasted if is do am I" Ajay yelled?

Jason looked at the woman with his eye brows raised?

"Well, do we make medicine lady or keep this senseless fighting up" Jazon asked?

The woman looked at Jazon in confusion and then Ajay as he jogged quickly up. She took a step closer to Ajay and inspected his eyes and then did the same to Jazon.

"Well, I'll be damned" The lady said!

The boys just looked at each other as if the lady was nuts. She was not nuts, just very well schooled as they would find out in a short time.

"Come with me boys, and give me back ma gaffe sonny" The old lady said with a chuckle.

The Shotgun was handed back over; although Ajay looked dubious about it. The lady walked toward a batch of weeds and disappeared suddenly.

"Are you coming or not" She yelled?

SHANE

"Why not" Ajay said?

Ajay was going to walk into the weeds first but Jazon who was less killable decided he should go first just in case the lady started blasting away. She did not. The weeds were not at all what they looked like. They were in fact a nice little cottage, perfectly camouflaged against intruders. Jazon walked in and stood by the little oak table and four matching hand carved chairs. Ajay went to sit down and the old woman turned on both of them with a torch and some hot water.

"What they hell are you? And you're the black boy, why are you traveling with a blood drinker, are his familiar" The old woman asked?

"Lady, who ever you are, I don't know what is going on with you, but Jazon is my best friend and has been since kindergarten. He only drinks animal blood from a butcher shop by the way. I don't know what you mean by familiar but I don't think that I am that" Ajay answered.

"I am Pegi" said the woman.

"I am Jazon, you already know I am a vampire, but I am unique. I am stronger, faster and I am immune to the things that other vampires can't stand. For example I wear a silver cross around my neck and go to church" Jazon said as he showed her his cross.

SHANE

"I knew there was something about you that was not right. My buckshot should have killed you as soon as it touched ya. You were hit, I am sure of it, but you do not seem to be even ill little alone dead. You're an amazing boy" Pegi said.

"Thanks. We are out here looking for some of my evil blood sucking cousins; that brought us to your door Pegi. Do you have any information that might help us bag that trash and get home faster" Jazon asked?

Pegi pondered the question for a tick and then pulled out a big flat bowl and filled it with water. She whipped out a knife cut her thumb and let three drops of blood fall into the water. She turned and handed the knife to Jazon.

"I need one drop of blood only from you into the water sonny" Pegi said.

Jazon cut himself under the thumb nail and let a single drop tap the still water in the basin. Pegi took the knife back and licked it clean. She looked a Jazon as she did it and smiled.

"You have the blood of heroes son, any how, here we go" Pegi said.

Pegi lit a cigar and puffed it three times and then she said a string of crazy words and on the last syllable she toss the cigar in the basin and the entire thing went to blaze.

"Show me where the vampires in the swamp are hiding" Pegi said?

The flames danced and then changed. Where the flames were now was a strange flamed picture of two black eyed men with dried blood on their faces and clothing. Both were handsome in a odd way, at least they would be without the blood all over the place. Pegi looked over the picture and then made a few hums, until the flames died out at last.

"What the hell was that Granny" asked? "Are you a witch or something"?

"Yes I am granny good witch; I look after the water ways out here. I thought you boys were those two; the ones you're after come here to eat ol' granny. I was ready for them, a little buck shot is their butt would have done it" Pegi said.

"They are vampires, what is buckshot going to do against them" Ajay asked?

"I use magic, wood, garlic and silver shot in every shell son, when a regular vampire gets hit with one of my loads; they go down and never get back up" Pegi explained.

That shut Ajay up, well for a moment.

"Hey, can I get a few of those Pegi. I am just a regular guy hunting vampires I can use all the help I can get" Ajay asked?

SHANE

Pegi smiled a big grin at him and then slapped his shoulder so hard it nearly flattened him. She was very strong it would appear.

"You can have ten and when those are gone, you come back and I will give you ten more. They are guaranteed to kill any vampire but him" Pegi said jerking a thumb at Jazon. "What is your story son"?

Jazon and Ajay filled Pegi in on everything for the next hour or so. She stopped them to ask questions on a few points but for the most part she puffed on a little pipe and listened.

"Wow; that is a pretty odd tale boys. I have not heard one like that in my two hundred and five years. You are some serious hunters and you're likely going to meet a bad ending, the brave at heart always do. Well, you may count old Pegi among your friends and allies kids" Pegi said.

"I am glad of it, you seem to have a lot of power and knowledge to share, not to mention some nifty ammo" Ajay commented.

"Stay here and get some chicken in you for the night and hunt during the day. We only saw two vampires in the bowl; that does not mean that is all there is. Magic is not an exact science so I don't want you to be surprised if you are out numbered when you finally catch up with them" Pegi told them.

Jazon and Ajay sat by the fire and listened to Pegi sin tales about the crazy life she has led. She told them her mother was a hedge witch and her father was part elf so she came to magic early in life. She lived alone because she did not like people messing with her karma or peace of mind. Frankly she was just plain weird and that bothered folks so it was easier for her not to have to deal with that. There was the fact that even though she was old, she never seemed to get any older or die, people tend to notice that. Pegi was really a very nice person, but lady-like would have been a stretch. Jazon and Ajay was glad that she was an old tomboy, it made talking to her about killing the vampires no biggy. Pegi was maybe 5'9, 175lbs, she had short cropped hair that was a seasoned pepper, and she wore a set of Mrs. Beasley glasses from the Family affair show, she smelled like flowers; although they were not sure which ones.

When morning came she gave them so food to take with them and sent them in the right direction to find their foe. When Pegi's island hideout was about an hour behind them Ajay decide to talk.

"She was really something else" Ajay said.

"Yeah, but considering all the new and wonderful people and creatures we have met lately. I mean come on your sleeping with a wood nymph, and Jax is sleeping with a vampire …me; our friends are witches, gnomes, and werewolves" Jazon said.

SHANE

The sun came up and Ajay could see the red begin to filter into Jazon's eyes; translation it was nearly show time. Ajay was tense but alert as they went along. Neither spoke, they knew that it was understood that silence would add to their personal security. It was not long after that when the hunters heard the first hints of voices ahead of them. It would appear that the prey did not know they were being hunted. But vampires were arrogant and that made them stupid, because Jazon and Ajay were going to kill them and burn their bodies very soon.

"Ready" Ajay confirmed as he checked to make sure there was a shell in the chamber and the safety was off on his shotgun.

"Me too" said Jazon.

Jazon let the boat slide up on to the beach and pulled out a short sword that looked like a cross. It was double sided and sharp and a straight razor, and 15 inches long. Ajay blinked when Jazon pulled it out from the small of his back, he had never seen it before.

"A gift from Tad, blessed by Father Sully" Jazon said to the unasked question.

"Kay" Ajay said.

It was just as Pegi had said, there were a lot more vamps than the few she saw in the bowl. Ajay made a pissy face as to say "no shit, I should have known". Jazon walked up around the short squat building; so

SHANE

that he could get behind the vampires on their blind side. Jazon was trying to give Ajay a better chance. Jazon was too fast and could fight way to well to think he would get put down, but Ajay was a human and they vampires could probably smell him!

"OH SHIT" Jazon snarled!

As one all the vampires turned and sniffed the air, and then looked right at Ajay. He smiled and spoke loud.

"I came here to kick ass and chew bubblegum; and I just ran out of bubblegum" Ajay laughed out loud.

The closest vampire did not even hear the shot that ripped his head off his body. The four vampires standing near him were also down. Pegi's shell were the bomb, if they did not kill you then they put you down in horrible pain. Ajay jacked another shell into the chamber and started blasting everyone. Jazon saw the pattern of Ajay's work, and followed behind him. All the dead Jazon split in half and tossed their hearts in the swamp, the injury lost their heads and heart an instant later. Ajay only had ten shells and the vampires saw the light and spread out so Ajay could not down them as groups. One very smart fighter with dark well groomed hair and minty breath ran up and hit Ajay in the chest. As Ajay fell back he kicked the vampire in the nuts so he could not just bite him. Ajay was already rolling in the air to come up on his feet; he

SHANE

might be scared to death but now was not time to show that.

"Hows da nutz bro" Ajay asked as he pulled his dagger and took the vampires head off?

"STOP" yelled a fat blond vampire with yellow eyes!

There was only four vampires out of thirteen left alive, Ajay was outstanding today; a real machine. The vampires were actually afraid of him and they were not charging him at all, everyone that got close enough Ajay killed.

"Why you come up in here killing my clan boy. I did nothing to you or him. So why are you killing my family" Fatty asked?

"You're a chick. OMG you are nasty. Anyway, one or more of you killed some girls and tossed them in the swamp, well that is against my laws. I have come to kill you back, it is only fair" Jazon explained.

"What, it weren't us that done it, the hedge witch is the one you want" Fatty said.

The hunters looked at each other and smiled, it was Ajay that explained the humor.

"When there is evil around my boys eyes turn a pretty color, and it did not happen when we met the Witch boys, so you'll are lying your asses off" Ajay said.

Fatty as it turned out was tough as nails and did not want to die over much. The other vampires were not family, more likely crew. Fatty sent them at Ajay like mad dogs. Ajay was on the ground stabbing and kicking but pinned nonetheless. Fatty took on Jazon. She was very fast and about six hundred pounds, so when she rammed Jazon it knocked the stuffing out of him. Jazon was on the ground sword arm pinned and the Fatty vampire on his chest.

"Not so tuff now are you, I am going to enjoy killing your friend slowly while you watch" Fatty said as she drooled.

(Laughter).

The fat vampire was surprised when Jazon laughed loudly and heart felt with his eyes closed. She believed he had lost his mind; that is until he opened them. She gasped!

"You will not kill my friend or myself" Jazon said.

In one crisp movement the fatty vampire was dangling by her throat as the end of Jazon's left arm, while he twirled his sword in the right smiling at her.

"I am...well a super vampire and your all hosed" Jazon said as he cut the fatty vampire into very small pieces in less then five seconds.

SHANE

(SCREAM OF PAIN)

Ajay scream and Jazon heard a bone snap. In a blink Jazon was knocking the three vampires that had Ajay down flying. Ajay was bleeding a lot, he had claw makers on his face and chest, his left arm was broken; however he still had the dagger grasped in it. Jazon looked at him as he got to his feet. Ajay's face was so fierce it shocked Jazon, he did not seem to care that he was mangled; Ajay never took his eyes off the three living vampires. A fire so bright burst in Jazon's heart, he began to cry he was so moved by Ajay's valor. Jazon turned on the live one and snarled; his eyes were so white they looked translucent.

"You should run" Ajay said softly to the vampires.

Jazon move to fast to be seen by even the vampires, Ajay knew that Jazon was moving faster now than he ever did before; he was pushing himself in blind anger. Two bloodsuckers were ripped apart in a blur and set on fire, though Ajay did not know how.

(Snarl)

The sound came from just behind Ajay, the injured young black man did not even look, he just tossed the barrel over his shoulder at face height and said one word.

"Goodbye".

The last sound the vampire heard was the ratchet of the shell being shoved in the chamber, and then a blinding flash and then death.

Ajay stuck the shotgun between his shoulders where it goes and went into the shed, a moment later he came out with a can of gas. He poured gasoline over the entire compound and then tossed a match. Jazon picked up Ajay and ran to the boat. They cast off just as the entire island became an inferno.

(Later in the swamp).

Pegi saw what she thought was a motor boat coming with a huge wake behind it. As the sun was coming up she saw a small boat barely touching the water moving at an impossible speed.

When Jazon saw how bad off Ajay really was; he ripped his shirt and coat off and grabbed the oars instead of using the little motor. Jazon beat his back and his complete strength into making the little boat blast through the swamp. So fast was Jazon rowing that the boat never dipped and bounced; it just rode the top of the wake at 70mph. Ajay for his part was alert and smiling, he was proud of himself. He faced great odds, kept his head and put them in the dirt permanently, sure he was hurt but still alive and they were not.

Pegi was at the little dock when they flew in literally, she had to jump back because the wave would have flattened her if not for the fact that she made the wind blow to buffer it away suddenly. The boat landed soft as a babies kiss on the wood planks, and Jazon had Ajay in his arms and was moving to fast for Pegi to follow. A moment later Pegi herself was being carried at break neck speed. Jazon put her down beside her table and chairs.

"Sorry Pegi, but Ajay is in piss-poor shape and he needs your special help, if you don't mind" Jazon said.

Ajay had nearly bled to death and Jazon was not in a good mood. Ajay had larger sections of skin missing from his chest and arms and the broken left arm was twisted as well. For a strong black man Ajay was looking very ash or news print grey.

"My God what did you do stand still while the tortured you" Pegi asked in a huff?

"Hell no, we kicked that ass they whole time Granny" Ajay said weakly.

Pegi turned to Jazon and he shook his head and then he added a few choice words of his own.

SHANE

"Ajay took down most of them and finished about forty percent off himself. He dropped the rest at my feet and I finished the job. Even after they had him down he never stopped fighting or even called for help, he just handled his business until he could help me finish them, but he paid a terrible price for his brass" Jazon explained. "After he was all tore up like this he burned the island himself, with no help from me. This guy is all man all the time, bravest MO-FO I know".

Jazon would have said more but Ajay collapsed on to the floor. Jazon had him up and on the sturdy table in an instant. Pegi pulled out a straight razor and cut off what was left of Ajay's shirt and vest. The witch turned to cupboard and took out some jars. The first one she opened was pretty smelly and gooey looking; she chuckled and cleared her throat. She opened two more jars and suddenly found what she was looking for. She turned to Ajay and bitch-slapped him. His eyes snapped open and there was malice in them.

"Sorry sonny, but you have to be awake for this. I am going to heal you up very fast and it is going to hurt like Hell, so you have to hold still and deal with it as best you can for as long as you can, understand" Pegi told Ajay. "No touching Jazon, his skin will be new and you can't touch him because it will tear if you do".

Jazon nodded. Pegi started slowly rubbing a wildflower scented goop all over Ajay and not just where his injuries were; but all over his chest and arms. Pegi grabbed Ajay's arm with a strength impossible for an old lady and snapped his arm bones back together with the ease of someone who had done this many times before. She rolled Ajay on to his side and covered his back in the goop. When she was satisfied he was covered properly she began the chant a spell. It was all white magic, earth or elf charms, no evil stuff. Ajay was in incredible agony but he did not move or speak and show any hint of movement at all. It was two hours start to finish, when Pegi sat down and asked Jazon if he felt like a taste of the Rye. At first Jazon was confused, but Pegi did not make him guess, she pulled out a very fine crafted glass jug and poured two mugs full or the booze. Jazon took the offered mug and gave it a pull; even as a vampire it took his breath away, but it was very good and it warmed his heart and body very nicely. Pegi downed her cup and poured her full and topped off Jazon.

"You know sonny, I left the company of people because I don't fit in fifty seven years ago, but I can't sit on the sidelines now that hell hath come to my backyard. When you take the young fellow back, I am going to go with you if you don't mind, besides your going to need my ability to heal in the days ahead I should think" Pegi told him as she sipped her spirits.

"Yes by all means come along with us, Ajay will no doubt get all racked up again playing at being a hero; it is only him and Jax that hold my humanity in check. If one or both of them died, it would be all out war and I

SHANE

would burn the world to ashes in my anger" Jazon said with a flash of white through his eyes.

Pegi was a little worried, she had never seen so powerful of a vampire, even more dangerous was his resolve and dedication to his family and friends. Pegi was sure that Jazon was completely serious about destroying everything in anger, and that he was not boasting, he could actually do it. She also noted that there was not an ounce of evil in this young man.

"What the hell is that smell" Ajay said in a groggy voice?

Jazon smiled and looked at Pegi, and then he got up and walked over to look at his mangled friend. Ajay was already healing up nicely, most of his wounds were closed and soft pink scars took their place.

"I believe it is Pegi's homemade hooch little big brother, you want a taste, it will warm up you sock if you do" Jazon said. "Wait is that okay Pegi, it won't hurt him will it, I mean with the goop that is all over him now"?

"Heck no, give him a pull on it, it is good for you, there is magic in the liquor and well as flavor. It will likely speed up his healing and help him rest easier" Pegi explained.

Ajay took two big mouthfuls of the hooch and the look on his face was priceless, it was a cross between OMG and wow this is good. Jazon sat and talked with

SHANE

his friend and never left his side until Ajay drifted off into an exhausted sleep. Jazon pulled out Ajay's weapons, he cleaned and oiled them. He made sure the dagger was sharp and then he put Ajay's gear back. Jazon cleaned his own sword and sat looking at the swamp. Pegi retired for a short nap she said; short apparently was a subjective term, because she slept until the next morning, some sixteen hours. When she finally woke up she made a tea and hot bread breakfast and told Ajay to get up and off her table. Ajay was surprised to see he was well enough to do just that.

"Man, I am pretty hungry granny; you think I could talk you out of some food" Ajay said with a big white toothed grin?

"Go split some wood for the fire and the stove, fetch some water from the well for tea and tell the vampire he can relax your going to live. I think Jazon is thinking about not having you go hunting with his anymore, because you almost died and he can't take that" Pegi said.

Ajay limped out of the little home and saw Jazon sitting on a log facing the direction at where the vampire island was burnt up. There was still smoke rising after a whole day. Ajay pulled a small throwing knife that Jazon had given him, he had four and they were perfectly balanced for throwing. Ajay hurled it at Jazon's back, Jazon did not even move, Ajay began to

SHANE

panic thinking he just stabbed his best friend. Fast as lightning Jazon was standing beside Ajay holding his knife smiling.

"Did you think your clunky foot steps went without notice, talk about noisy, what an elephant, I am surprised you tried to pig-stick me though, bad form old man" Jazon said with a mock scowl?

Ajay laughed and elbow Jazon's chest.

"Jazon that was PHAT, you're fast as hell brother, I could not even see you move, I swear you still looked like you were on the log when you touched me. I am damn glad I am not your enemy" Ajay said.

"That could never happen little brother, we are like twins, we need to breath the same air, why else would you risk your life following me here and everywhere I go" Jazon said.

Ajay cleared his throat, he could see that Jazon was swimming in guilt and did not want to go down that path just now. Some arguments need to be planned out and this was one of those.

"Hey Pegi is making some grub boy and we need to make some other these logs smaller so they can find their way into her stove and we can get fed" Ajay said.

Jazon knew his friend was stalling because he could feel Jazon's distress over his Ajay's injuries and near miss with the reaper. Jazon decide this was not the time to have a BF over things.

SHANE

Ajay lead Jazon to the log Pegi was using for stove fire wood and snatched up an axe and was about to have at it, when Jazon stopped him.

"Hold on a tick mate" Jazon said with a smile.

Jazon stepped up to the log and stood it up long way and ripped it in half and then ripped the halves into quarters, and then eighths. Ajay just watched amazed once again and Jazon's show of incredible strength.

"Nice" Ajay said.

Ajay reached over and took Jazon sword off his back and smiled at Jazon.

"My turn to amaze you brother" Ajay said. "Hold the log parts back together again standing up".

Jazon did as he was asked, when he was in position he told Ajay to go ahead and do what ever he had in mind. Ajay smiled and in a zigzag motion he cut the wood into small pieces in two seconds with Jazon sword. Jazon smiled.

"Damn, I need to get you one of those to carry; you're a thug with that in your grasp" Jazon said.

The boy carried in a lot of wood for the fire and Pegi looked at the wood that was custom cut and smiled at the skills the boys displayed openly. The meal was superb, Pegi could cook up a storm and the tea though oddly seasoned and spiked was equally as enchanting. They ate a lot of food and three pots of tea; and not the tiny girlie pots either; the big industrial **FOLGERS** stainless steel coffee pot kind. When Pegi was sure the boys were full she simply said a short phrase.

"Clean thy self cookware and be in yer appointed place, if you please" Pegi said.

The dishes jumped into the sink washed, dried and put themselves away. All by themselves, if the boy had forgot that this was the house of a witch; it all came back suddenly to them now. Pegi looked at them and she became suddenly much younger.

"Oh come on fella's how did you think I lived so long? That hooch as you call it is an eternal life potion. You only have to drink it every so often to continue on your way. You both drank it, so you will both be young for at least another fifty or sixty years" Pegi told them.

"Can I get a bottle of that for Jax, I love her and would like her to stay hot and young as well" Jazon asked?

"No, you should turn her" Pegi said as she looked around the home.

Instantly Jazon looked crestfallen. Pegi noticed. Ajay was about to speak but the young fit Pegi pulled her dress off and stood there naked. She was fit and damn fine physically, Ajay whistled at her nude body. She smiled and opened a drawer and took out a sexy set of sheer underwear and put them on, then some hiking short and a baseball jersey. She looked like a twenty something girl ready for a summer day, not a 205 year old woman.

"Jazon trust me, if you love her and she wants to have you turn her, then no evil will be passed, the change will take place from love not force, that will make all difference" Pegi explained.

In a whirl wind of movement the boys were ushered out the door; and Pegi turned and snapped her fingers and her entire home was the size of a walnut in the palm of her hand. She smiled at the boys who were wide eyed at the sight of it all.

"This is the only way to pace your shit" Pegi said.

The old turn young again witch turned and walked to the beach away from the side of her island they were on. She snapped her fingers and a schooner popped out of a bottle into the swamp. It was okay though the damn swamp was man made and twenty feet deep. The ship was smaller than the big ocean cousin, but it was a mighty vessel and gorgeous.

"All aboard matey; it is time to sail this baby to the port and get your car and ride the wind northward home" Pegi said all excited.

They all got aboard and Pegi took over the sail jumped open and caught the wind and the ship danced on the water like a ballerina. The hunters had rowed for hours to get to where they wanted to be in the swamp, but the schooner raked across the delta in nothing flat and Pegi was the Flying Dutchman at the helm.

Jazon yelled that he mustang was off the side right in the dirt near the small private boat launch. Pegi told Ajay to take the wheel and she came to stand by Jazon at the rail, she reached out her hand and whispered something Jazon did not understand and the cars was tiny and in her hand the next instant.

"Here don't loose this, and don't worry about the oil and gas won't leak while the car is in stasis" Pegi explained as she handed the car to Jazon.

VAMPIRE HERO SAGA

SHANE

CHAPTER 7: FINNEY COMETH

Brian Finney was not a kind man even before he was turned, you might say he was a prick. However, Mark O'Day seemed to love him and worship the ground he walked on. Which is odd considering Mark's maternal grandfather is Collin O'Day. Collin is the ruler of all of Europe, he lives in Ireland and is by all rights and deeds the king of the island through blood line as well as by strength of his sword arm. Collin is not anything like Mark. Mark is trash; Collin is a man's man and a gentleman to boot.

"Mark come here and explain again how you were unable to kill this man in time. He is proving to be a pain in me arse of late. I am not sure I want him dead yet, but it is in me mind lad" Brain said with a flourish.

"The sun came up as I was finishing him; the damned kid was not as easy to put down as I had hoped. I went back to finish him up and his black steward hit me with a bat. The boy himself has turned and is faster and stronger than I am, he may be your match in strength, but he is definitely faster than you are my Lord" Mark said.

"Indeed" Brian commented. "I have heard of his insane speed and amazing strength, one might think he has old blood in his veins to be granted this boon".

SHANE

Finney walked over to his desk and typed in a code. The wall safe opened up and mark turned and looked in it. He was always amazed to see Brian's outrageous wealth. Inside the walk-in safe were stacks of hundred dollar bills into the millions, stacks of gold bars, and stacks of platinum bars in the back. Brain Finney was called the Prince of Portland, but he ruled the west coast and he could buy the country and pay the national debt off with what was just in this safe here, Brian had many more safes with even greater wealth within.

"Mark, grab two stacks of hundreds and go get Gilly to kill this up-start and his black follower dead. The cash is for Gilly, he knows how much his is to be paid, do not mess with him. Gilly is old and mean, his only true love is murder" Brian scolded Mark.

"I got it Brain, I am not one for bringing the nutter Gilly on me own head for any reason" Mark said.

"See that you don't for your sake. Now go on get this done and then join me for dinner at the club" Brian said with a smile.

Mark took the cash, about one hundred thousand large and walked out and took the stairs down to ground level. Mark did not like elevators or escalators either. Brian closed the vault and then sat at his desk smiling at the stairs where Mark just left. Brain genuinely adored Mark, like a little brother. He knew one day Mark would mess up back enough he might have to kill him for the greater good, but it would be a dark day for Brian when it final came.

(Later at Gilly's home).

Mark knocked on Gilly's door softly; because the killer did not like anything more than killing and less than excessive noise. Gilly opened the door and looked upon Mark with open disdain until Mark opened his over coat and showed Gilly the money.

"Come in" Gilly said in a barbwire voice.

A long time ago Gilly crossed the wrong man and got his own throat cut, it made Gilly's voice raspy and rough. Soon after being turned, Gilly hunted down the man who gave him his famous voice and cut his throat and let him drown in blood over a week's time. Gilly was not to be messed with.

"Who is the bloody target this time" Gilly inquired.

"A newly turned vampire and his black shadow" Mark said.

"FLEDGLINGS, I am to be wasted on fledglings; why does Finney not send you to kill these infants" Gilly snarl in anger?

"I made the vampire by accident and have tried to remedy the error but, this infant is stronger and faster than I, and he has caused Brian a great pain in the arse lately so he must be killed and you are the best at that kind of business" Mark explained.

Gilly looked at Mark and sized him up. Mark was not a bad ass, but he was not a wussy either. If the new vampire could not be killed by Mark at his early stage of development, he did indeed need to be killed before he grew up and came into his true strength.

"What is his name and where I find him" Gilly asked.

Mark explained everything to Gilly, and then he left in a hurry. Gilly goes into a kind of lunatic trance, and he amps up until he kills his victim. Gilly is covered in scars, he has been cut up a thousand times and he has come close to dying while attempting to kill a prey. Still, Gilly has never known defeat.

Gilly knew Mark was scared of him; Brian however was not and for good reason. Gilly was a ruthless killer, but Brian was peerless in combat, a natural slayer. Brian was so good his body did not have a single scar on it. What this meant in a nutshell was; Gilly had better kill these fledglings or Gilly might be the next target. Brian had a soft spot for only Mark; all others were expendable as fodder as far as Gilly knew.

Gilly decided he would go observe the prey and maybe kill him unaware and then he would torture his shadow for a week or so. The thought brightened Gilly's heart. Yes Gilly was a sick puppy.

SHANE

(At the Finney's club)

There were three beautiful human girls sitting with Brain when Mark arrived clean shaven and well dressed for dinner. Mark was a jeans and shirt guy, however no matter how close he was with Brian; Mark dare not come to dinner unwashed and below Brian's standard of public dress standard. Brian bought and paid for Mark's tailored clothing to be sure Mark was presentable for elegant company at dinner. Brian was a two face as Mark called them. It was not an insult, more of an accurate description. It meant that Brian acted like a human in public, hiding what he really was, and was a complete monster in private. Brian actually liked the title of two face, it meant he was maintaining his façade of humanity perfectly.

"Good evening Brian and ladies" Mark said with a small bow.

The girls giggled at Mark's formal tone and suave manner. Mark was trashy by nature but could act the part of a gentleman easily if he wanted to. When he went out for the night with Brian he got to practice this act often enough that is was seamless.

"Well meet Markus, come sit my friend, enjoy this fine company" Brian said indicating the young ladies.

"Thank you, I believe it will" Mark said as he sat down.

SHANE

One of the things that Mark like more than sex and almost as much as the taste of fresh healthy blood was watching Brian work a room and then bed any woman he wanted. Most of the time Brian did not kill his lovers, he said it would lead to his door and humans might be physically weak but their minds were to damn sharp to be stupid around them. Brian danced with every one of the young ladies and he kissed them all on the lips as if they were the only person in the room. Mark usually ended up with one a the girls at the end of the night, it did not matter which one they were always gorgeous, Brian never dated or dined with anyone who was less than breath taking.

After a fine meal and some fooling around, Brian and Mark met back at Finney's office downtown.

"Did you enjoy your evening Mark" Brian asked/

"You know I did Brian, you are the best host ever and a great friend & lord" Mark answered.

Brian looked up from his work and smiled at Mark, who was sucking up as usual. Brian knew that with mark he meant it, even if it was a bit of sucking up. Oh, well on to business.

"Did Gilly seem like he was going to get right on the job, or was he in a loafing mode when you were there" Brian asked?

Mark closed his mind in reflection, trying to draw up the entire meeting and replay it in his head. He

SHANE

remembered Gilly was peeved at first, then after a short explanation of how the enemy came about he seemed to almost be intrigued if that was possible for Gilly.

"He was unpleased at first, even angry that his talents were being wasted. He however came around when I told him how fast the fledgling is" Mark explained.

"I see; Gilly was right to be pissed; he is after all an artist when it comes to killing. He will be on our young friends trail even now I believe. Gilly will not fail, his pride would not allow it" Brian said.

"He makes my skin crawl, that voice of his is vile

It makes you want to despise him and I do. If you ever decide to end your association with him, I would gladly sever the ties for you" Mark explained.

Brian only smiled, Mark really would wipe Gilly off the planet, sure Gilly was tougher and mad in the head, however; Mark would find a way to finish Mr. Gilly off cleanly.

(3AM in front of Jazon's old condo)

Gilly sat on the curb watching the fledgling's home waiting for him to come home or his black shadow to slide by so at the least Gilly could size them up for the kill if not snuff them right there and then. Jazon never came home, nobody came to visit and some old bat kept looking out the window every few minutes at him. Gilly could care less, if she came out side she was a snack, if not then she might live to annoy someone else later on.

Jazon did not live there anymore, and Gilly was misinformed by Mark, which was going to get him into some bother with Gilly later. Ajay therefore, was not going to come there, heck nobody would. Gill finally got up and left forty minutes before the sun came up, he went to find Mark to thrash him for wasting his time. That was at least some consolation thought with a twisted smile.

(On the Columbia River came a schooner).

Ajay was practically Black beard the pirate by the time Pegi got him in the groove of the ship. Ajay loved sailing this sleek razor of a ship through the water, it glided as if on air and it was as fast as a power boat; enchanted thought Ajay, no doubt. Jazon watched Pegi as she slept, they had bonded like very close brother and sister. Pegi as a young woman was HOT, but Jazon and Ajay knew she was really old in years and her mind was strong and vast. You could not court this woman unless you really had your head on right and your A game on. Neither Jazon nor Ajay wanted to push up on

SHANE

her, despite her hotness because they already had a hot woman in their lives and hearts. Beside Pegi might punish them if they tried to steal some pooty.

"Hey I am getting a little puckish Jazon, how about some grub bro" Ajay called down the hold?

Pegi opened her eyes and looked at Jazon's beautiful face. Pegi slept nude and her young hard body was a fine sight indeed. Pegi sat up and jumped on Jazon's lap, she kissed him softly.

"You hungry to tiger" Pegi asked?

"Yes, but not for food Pegi" Jazon said as he patted her bare butt.

Pegi smiled pretty big.

"I had forgotten what it is to have desire and be desired by another. It feels good, but you really don't want me that way do you" Pegi asked?

"If not for Jax, yes I would want you that way Pegi, but alas I love her, so I will hold my water until I can hold her in my arms again" Jazon said.

Pegi kissed him again playfully and then gave him a serious look.

"You are a good man you know, she is damn lucky to have your love, I hope she knows that" Pegi said seriously.

"Ask her when you meet her" Jazon said.

The meal Pegi whipped up was excellent as always, the boys ate and ogled Pegi who was still buck naked. She seemed to relish the attention and she was not a bit modest or embarrassed. She decided to final get dressed after breakfast when Ajay was bringing the ship into dock which sent the dock patrons on their ear seeing a schooner rolling in with no wind.

"Okay boys let's go to town" Pegi said.

They all left the schooner and stood on the dock, Pegi turned and whistled softly and the schooner disappeared. She grabbed Ajay and pulled him closer to her, she wrapped her other arm around Jazon's waist and the three of them walked up the stairs to the parking lot, where Pegi asked for Jazon's mustang. Jazon pulled his car out of his jeans pocket and handed it over. Pegi tossed it into the air low over the ground and snapped her fingers; it landed full size in the road just in front of them. She smiled.

The ride to the Paradice club where Jazon lived went quick, mostly because Jazon had a foot made out of pure lead-onium. Pegi loved the way Jazon drove; she was all tomboy when it came to speeding and being reckless. Ajay was a tad green around the gills by the time they pulled up into the private parking spot reserved for Jazon.

Enoch was in the shadows watching them, Jazon's eyes turned red instantly and Ajay pulled his shotgun in a blur, and they both knew they were not alone. Pegi just pointed into the shadows right at Enoch. Jazon saw him before she pointed, but Jazon did not drop his guard, it could be a fake out and they could be in trouble.

"JAZON"!

A sexy red haired girl in baggy shorts and a bikini top jumped into Jazon's arm and stuck her tongue in his mouth and wrapped her leg around his body like a vine. She would not let go for anything. She was turning blue from holding her breath. Jazon finally pulled his breathless lover away enough to look at her. He smiled so big and genuine that she was back on him the next instant.

Ajay walked up to the Giant bald black man Enoch and gave him an elbow tap.

"Everything quiet while we were gone" Ajay asked?

"Not a peep" Enoch answered, "Good hunting"?

"We found them and put them down, all of them" Ajay said.

Enoch sniffed him and his eyebrows rose. The Giant leaned down and inspected ajay more closely.

"Seems that you nearly did not make it home again young man, you smell like blood, your own, if my eyes did not say you are well; then my nose would say you should be near death with injuries" Enoch?

"You're not human" Pegi said.

SHANE

Enoch jumped because she was touching him and he did not know she was there. It is common knowledge that you cannot sneak up on a Werewolf, their sense are to acute, yet Pegi just did and it scared Enoch. He just looked down at the goddess running her hands over his huge muscular body. She was beautiful and fit as a warrior.

"No, I am not, not for a great long time" Enoch said. "Who are you, what are you"?

Pegi smiled and leaned on Enoch and listened to his mighty heart beat, Enoch could not help himself; he put his arms around her affectionately, so why was he reacting to her this way. Enoch was a loner for the most part, but this woman had his heart pounding and his head reeling. It was not just her beauty, it was everything about her, and she was like a drug to Enoch's senses, her touch, her smell and body, her gaze made Enoch feel high.

"You are very strong and so very lonely my huge friend. I will be your light in the dark, and perhaps more if we find we want to explore that path" Pegi said.

"I am a werewolf" Enoch said in his bass voice.

Pegi jumped back and hissed at him. Enoch wanted to take a defensive position but he just could not bring himself to want to attack her, so he just stood there looking miserable. Pegi suddenly looked as if she

SHANE

would cry. She jumped into Enoch mighty arms; he caught her gently and cradled her body to his.

"I am sorry, I was playing. I could feel you heart crush in your chest from despair and I could feel you pain physically. I will never do that to you again. I want to be your close friend and heal you injured soul Enoch" Pegi said.

"I...would ...like that" Enoch managed to say.

"I am a part Elf hedge witch; I am 205 years old just so you know" Pegi told him.

Enoch put her down and looked her over and chuckled.

"You have a great ass for an old lady" Enoch laughed.

The five friends went in to the club and had a beer and some lunch.

VAMPIRE HERO SAGA

SHANE

CHAPTER 8: ASSASSINS

The night of their return Jazon and Ajay met with Father Sully and Tad. The afternoon was spent making love to the women who loved them and that was something neither man wanted to rush. Silky was so overjoyed that Ajay was back she didn't notice how injured Ajay was until round three of love making. Then she asked, when Ajay explained the story Silky's face went white and she looked ill, and then she cried hard. Ajay comforted her until she calmed down.

"I almost lost you and I just found you" Silky said.

Ajay just smothered her in love and soon she forgot everything but the moment.

Jax had a lot of built up sexual aggression, it was a good thing Jazon was a vampire or she might have hurt him during her sexual aerobics. Jazon could not have been any more happy. Jax asked about the sexy girl that came back with them and whether Ajay or Jazon had bedded her? Jazon told her all about Pegi and that he most definitely not bone Pegi, though she was hot and desirable, she was not in Jax league as a woman in his opinion, he loved Jax and would not be screwing anyone she did not want him to. Jax was not a jealous woman, and she may or may not be into sharing at

SHANE

some point but she wanted Jazon all to herself for now and it seemed that Jazon was with that program.

(Later at Father Sully's church)

Tad and Wolf were waiting for Jazon to arrive. Ajay and Silky were in the corner and she was still very angry with Ajay and Jazon for getting he big chocolate daddy messed up. Ajay had snuggled her enough that she was pretty milk-toast about it at this point. Jazon pulled up in his mustang and Jax got out of the passengers side, Jazon jumped out and back flipped over the car and closed her door for her as his feet touched the ground beside her.

"Show off" Jax giggled as her arm slipped around his waist.

The two lovers walked into the church and sat down among their friends. Jax and Silky who were nursing a budding friendship began to chat each other up about recent events. Most of the assembly had never met Jax. She was a sight, her hard muscular body and short bright red pixie hair cut, with her pale piercing green eyes, she was stunning and of-course she wore a tiny mini skirt and a skin tight tank top without a bra. Needless to say it brought the animal out in everyone who saw her, they only stayed away

SHANE

because Jazon would kill anyone who touched her, and this much was common knowledge.

"What's new Mick" Jazon asked.

It was Tad who answered with a grim face. It was always odd to think of the extremely cute gnome as the leader of the rebellion.

"Finney has put an assassin on you, Ajay, Silky and Jax" Tad said flatly.

"What, I get going after us, but not the girls. That is some bullshit right there" Ajay said.

It seemed like the room was holding their breath waiting for Jazon and all his strength to blow up. He just sat there thinking calmly while Ajay ranted a bit.

"Who is it and where can I find them" Jazon asked?

"It is a nutter call Gilly. He may be mad in the head but he is no second rate killer, if he is after you Finney wants you dead badly, because Gilly has never missed" Wolf said.

"Do you boys know where he is or not" Jazon asked in a low tone?

The group was aware of how deeply angry Jazon was not by his tone but because his eyes were pale pink and turning whiter all the time. Tad was about to speak when Father Sully stopped him with a hand on his shoulder.

SHANE

"What are you going to do son if you know where he is to be found" Mick asked?

(Laughter from Ajay and Jazon).

"I am going to go face him and put him into the ground personally and burn his remains, I am going to toss his head and heart on Finney's lap; so the next time he thinks of sending someone after me he will need to think again" Jazon said in a deadly calm voice.

Even Ajay shook with a sudden chill, so cold was Jazon's statement that everyone could feel in physically. However, Ajay looked as ready to go as Jazon did, so did some of the others.

"I need to know that Jax and Silky are safe while we deal with this trash" Jazon said.

"I will look after the girls; you know I am up to it. If any of them blood sucker or anything else comes my way I will shrink them and put them in a box" Pegi laughed!

Pegi gave most of the creatures and fairy folk the jeebs. She was powerful and off beat, she seemed a white witch but they were still leery of her, she was much to flip about the use of her magic. Tad and a few others were magic users as well and Pegi; in Tad's opinion could beat all of them put together if push came to shove. Only Jazon seemed to be able to stand against her. Pegi noticed the gnome staring at her and spoke as if she could read his mind, which she could. Handy no?

"I would never trade my friendship with the boys for anything; they have proved themselves to me to be pure of heart and fierce in combat, and loyal to the bone. If you stand by their side then I am your friend, if you oppose them I am your enemy Tad. I am extremely powerful, and immortal, if you wish for me to teach your magic users more powerful forms of magic then I will; but have care never to cross me, I am not forgiving in any way, shape or form" Pegi addressed Tad thoughts.

Tad blanched, Wolf smiled and Ajay laughed openly at the look on the tiny gnomes face. Enoch put his massive hand on Pegi's shoulder gently and gave a little grip. He was letting her know he trusted her and would have her back if need be. Enoch had few friends and Pegi was not one he would loose easily, she made him feel like man and more.

"Enough of this foolishness, where is the assassin hiding" Jazon said sternly?

The rest of the even was spent coordinating how they would catch the killers off guard and not get killed themselves. Enoch told Pegi that no vampire could get close enough to her to hurt her; it was true in wolf form Enoch had never lost a battle to a vampire. Ajay and Biz were in the corner. The silent young man listened and Ajay spoke and shook his head every so often but did not speak as usual. Ajay shook Biz's hand and walked back to where Silky was. Jazon had Father Sully bless him and all his weapons, then he had the good father Bless the entire company and all their weapons as well. Only Pegi abstained, she said that it might interfere with her earth magic to be blessed, not that she did not love God, it was actually quite the opposite.

(ELSEWHERE LOOMING IN THE SHADOWS)

Gilly finally had a lead on Jazon, he found the club, Paradice how the opposite it would turn out for his prey. Gilly watched people going in and out, mostly young women. Gilly was not a social creature by nature, he liked to kill, than pretty much capped any friendships. Although Gilly was know to have a lover or two and he never killed them, it was one of the few things he would not do. If a woman was willing to pleasure him and be pleasured by him, then he would not harm them at all. The scores of hot young women going into the club set Gilly's desire for a new companion off. After he killed his prey he would have to find a new lover and take a vacation to somewhere remote and far away from this life. Most of the girls he had been with over the years did not know he was a vampire and he kept it that way, to them he was just an eccentric man of wealth. Yes I need a vacation Gilly thought to himself. Gilly was jerked out of his pondering when a mustang pulled up and his prey got out.

"Stay in the car Jax, we are not alone" Jazon said handing Jax a pistol from his pocket. "If anything gets by me shoot them, the gun has Pegi's special rounds and they have been blessed and dipped in holy water".

Jazon got out and looked around, instantly he found Gilly's face in the dark. Gilly did not want to fight Jazon heads up, he wanted ambush him and kill him easily, but the choice was about to be taken away from him. Jazon moved so fast even Gilly's trained eyes lost him until Gilly was wrench off his feet and slammed into the ground like a Mack truck hit him. Gilly pulled a knife and tried to stab Jazon, but Jazon just slapped the knife out of his hand and broke the offending arm that held it.

"Listen to me coward, if you want me, come for only me, if you harm anyone but me, I wont kill you, I will pull your arms and legs off and burn them while you watch, then I will stake you out butt naked in the sun and watch you roast everyday for a year, so you die slowly, painfully" Jazon snarl in Gilly's face.

Gilly was afraid of nothing as a rule, but this fledgling was terrifying, his every word spoke of death and pain and he meant each word truly. Gill was not

SHANE

ready for this one. So he made up his mind to lie his way out.

"I am only a watcher, a scout, I am not the enemy. I will tell my master you words if you let me live" Gilly lied.

"Fine, tell him or them that I am not playing, if I see any of you near my family it will be the slow death. One more thing, you tell Finney personally I am going to take his head off, he should have never sent an assassin after me, now it is my turn" Jazon said as he yanked Gilly off the ground hurled him down the alley.

Gilly rolled came up on his feet and was running at top speed away from the mad fledgling. How could a fledgling be so strong or fast. Gilly would kill him, but for once Gilly was going to not work alone. Gilly only stopped running after he was in uptown Portland, where he knew some seedy low rent vampire hung out. Gilly walked into the bar and looked around; by the eyes Gilly could identify several of his kind. Gilly walked over and sat among a group of seven. They looked at him with mild interest.

"You boys want to make some easy money" Gilly asked?

"What you got in mind Gilly" Said a black haired Vampire with a scar over one eye?

SHANE

"Murder what else, but it is only humans you will be after, I will deal with their guardian myself" Gilly answered.

The black haired vamp was named Tony and Tony lead this little murder squad. They were low rent but professional in their work, they would be cheap by Gilly's standard but what ever the cost, worth the money thought Gilly.

"What is the offer for the job" Tony asked?

"That depends on what you are willing to do" Gilly answered honestly.

"We will do whatever is required to get paid, if the job calls for slaughter then we will do that, or surgical kills we can do that as well. You tell me the job and I will request what I think the work is worth, is that acceptable" Tony asked?

Gilly smiled he liked Tony; here was a vampire he could deal with. Gilly pondered for a moment just what he wanted to say to Tony about the work, he made up his mind and spoke.

"I am going to lure a group of people to a ambush and I want your crew to make sure nobody gets away. Do not under estimate the prey they are not lackluster kills, they will fight back expertly and some of you crew may be killed; with that said name your price" Gilly announced.

"A moment to confer with the boys" Tony said.

SHANE

The group got up and left out the front door and onto the roof across the street. Tony watched for Gilly.

"That is Gilly the famous Vampire assassin, he works alone. If he is hiring us to play a part it is likely a very dangerous game he plays and we are to be wasted in the fruition of his goal" Tony said.

"So you think he is holding back some information or just plain lying" A vamp said.

"Of-course he is lying his ass off, if he told us his was really after that Vampire hunter we would not go alone with it" Tony said.

"Vampire hunter"?

"Yes, there are only two people I can think of that Gilly could not kill head to head, Brian Finney, which Gilly is a long term employee and the new Vampire hunter who has been killing entire clans and families by himself. The new hunter is a super predator, and if we encounter this hunter we will surely die. So before we take this job each of us must be willing to gamble our lives away for monetary gains" Tony said.

Tony looked around and regarded each of the members of his crew and they all looked ready to take the job to Tony.

"Is there nobody opposed" Tony asked?

"We live a great long time Tony and boredom is a foe that is harder to beat than others. I for one will risk it all not for the money but for the exhilaration of the fight itself. I want to feel something again, even if it is pain" one of the crew said.

"So be it, we take the job. Let us go back down and close the deal with Gilly" Tony said.

Gilly was not surprised that they came back and was less surprised when they all sat back down grim faced. It said to Gilly they were in.

"Gentlemen what is your decision" Gilly asked?

"We are in, we will take the job. We want fifty grand per man, and we want half up front as a show of good will, not to mention if we get killed you keep the other half" Tony said.

"Very true, I agree to your price and will have your money here tomorrow night, as the sun will be up before I could retrieve your money and be back here safely" Gilly said.

Gilly got up and walked out, he laughed to himself as he walked through the shadows toward his home. He was not followed, nobody was that stupid and if they were, then a late snack was no hassle to Gilly, he was a vampire after all.

(Two days later).

SHANE

Pegi woke up in her huge four poster bed, she was nude as usual. She tossed the covers off and walked to the door and opened it, Enoch was sitting in a chair guarding her door. He looked up at her nude body; this was the second morning she had shown off her magnificent figure. Enoch reached out and lifted Pegi into his arms and she kissed his neck and she put her head on his massive shoulder. Pegi could hear the content rumble deep in Enoch chest.

"Why don't your ever share the bed with me Enoch, even if you don't want to have sex, it is better than this damn chair at night. I can behave myself" Pegi said.

"I am afraid I will loose control and kill you in a fit of lustful passion. I am just not strong enough yet to be than close to you in that way. I will have to work up to it, if you are still willing by the time I can handle the power of my feelings" Enoch said in a low baritone voice.

"No hurry, I am an old witch down deep my huge friend. I am not running off anywhere, but I might get some desires of my own so don't wait to long or Pegi my have to have a little something on the side while I am waiting for the main course" Pegi said teasingly.

Enoch was not use to having anyone tease him or flirt with him, and here was a goddess actually seducing him and treating him like a man, her man. He liked it and he wanted her in the worst way, but he was driven by wild emotions and he lost control much to easily for him to couple with her. What he did not know was, Pegi had no intention of bedding another man, she was an old woman in a young woman's body. She loved being a little trampy, but she was not a tramp or a ho, she was just super playful whether young or old.

"Come on big boy, let's go get something to eat. Do you want me to cook for you" Pegi asked?

Since Pegi arrived at the safe house which was an old hotel that Tad and Silky had renovated, Pegi had done a great deal of cooking and everyone could not be more happy with that. Pegi Was a master chef, she cooked things that did not sound good until you put them in your mouth and then you knew, you were oh so wrong to question Pegi's chow. Enoch tossed Pegi into the shower and towel dried her body. Pegi grabbed a yellow summer dress that was cut off to her lean thighs and pulled her giant wolf friend after her to the amazing stainless steel kitchen where she made dreams come true. The Kitchen was always clean. Living with earth spirits, faeries and sprites has the advantage of type A cleaners, they can't stand a mess or filth, so everything in the hotel was spotless.

"Bacon, flour, eggs, maple, butter, and strawberries, I need these things for this mornings bounty. Girls, girls up and at'em" Pegi yelled.

Four gorgeous winged faeries fluttered down the hall, each hugged Pegi in their gentle way. She

SHANE

explained the plan for the meal and the girls, went to gather the berries for Pegi, Enoch took care of the Bacon. Jazon who had a good thing going with a fine local butcher always kept the meat locker full of good quality meat, the best most the werewolves ever had. Jazon and Ajay also kept the pantry full and the fridge packed with fresh organic veggies for the non-meat eaters. Enoch thought God blessed them all the day Jazon walked into the warehouse where they had hidden for a month, Ajay was just as good; he was using the wealth from his football career to support all the magical creature's lives.

"Heads up Enoch, we are cooking not daydreaming. Now hand me that meat" Pegi said and she started the cooking dance she did every morning.

Enoch believed it was a form of martial arts he decided, because when she had knives in her hands she was deadly and precise. The faeries came back with strawberries and raspberries as well all large and plump, they were very pleased with the bounty.

Three hours after Pegi started she ate her little meal with her kitchen helpers and Enoch. They laughed and sang and enjoyed the moment. It would be nice if it could last forever; but that is a foolish thought...

CHAPTER 9: PLAY BALL

In the seedier part of town just after sundown a deadly predator dropped his latest victim to the ground dead, drained of the precious life giving fluid we call blood. The predator decide to have some mercy so they carried the body out to the street un-mutilated and left it for the police to find so they could bury the body and the family could have closure. This was actually not unusual for Gilly, he liked to fight a victim and then kill them. This poor soul was just food and they could not put up a fight, they gave in to their fate. Gill promised them no real pain and so he made a small laceration and drained them painlessly to death. The man simply fell into a stupor, then finally a silent death.

"Good luck in the next life Mate" Gilly said "May the sea bring you riches and the adventure your heart yearned for".

Gilly loved the sea, he was a sailor by nature and trade. He knew more about the oceans of our planet than most oceanographers do, he could sail by scent alone and the roll of the sea. Gilly respected the sea and the strength of it. When Gilly finally meets his reward; his last wish is a burial at sea. As far as charity goes, Gilly actually has some. He respects

SHANE

courage even in the weak; that is why he did not make the man suffer and why he put him where he could be found and carried for. Gilly hated stupidity though and false pride even more. Arrogance he liked because it made the targets fall so much more profound when he took them down. Anyway Gilly was heading to see Tony and the gang to pay them and set Jazon up for the kill. Gilly was excited.

"In a few day fledgling you will be my bitch"!

Tony and his band were watching for Gilly and knew he was near before he actually arrived. Tony had stayed alive almost as long as Gilly by never being unprepared. Tony was not as tough as Gilly but he was close and he never let on that he was a superior vampire in any way; if he did Brian Finney would have him killed before he gained to large a following. Brian Finney was not one to take chances with his precious power. Tony had his little band of followers and than is all he ever wanted.

The bar door opened and in walked Gilly with a bowling bag in his left hand and a bowie knife in his right. Tony and the others; were on guard the moment they knew Gilly was coming. Now they were thinking perhaps they were the target here. But Tony did not seem worried over much so they settled down. Tony had a crossbow over his lap and was looking unblinking at Gilly.

"Hail Gilly, how are you this fine day" Tony inquired?

SHANE

They vampires could smell the fresh blood on Gilly and knew he was strong and well fed just now, they also were well fed just incase this turned ugly suddenly. Gilly was a notorious killer, you could not take anything for granted around him.

"I am well thank you, and I have brought your funding in the amounts you requested Tony" Gilly said pleasantly.

"What is the big knife for Gilly, this is business after all or are we the business" Tony asked?

Gilly genuinely looked surprised; he saw the bowie knife in his hand and laughed. He slipped it back up under his jacket and removed his hand.

"I beg your pardon, I used it a short while ago and I guess I never put it away absent mindedly. I am not here to hunt you, I would tell you openly" Gilly said.

Tony put his crossbow on the table and looked at Gilly closely and he shook his head. It was true Gilly was a straight up killer; he would want you to know ahead of time that he came for you so you knew who took your life away. Tony made a sweeping motion toward the chair in front of him. Gilly walked forward placed the bag on the table and then sat down. One of Tony's guys took the bag off the table so Tony could see clearly. He did not however open the bag and count it, that would have been very rude and possibly fatal.

SHANE

"So Gilly what is your plan for the target and how do you wish for us to assist you in your game" Tony asked in just the right words?

Gilly smiled and Tony's wise chose of words and the crossbow was prudent as well considering Gilly was involved. Gilly made a mental note to re-examine Tony, he was not a low level flunky, he was a sleeper. Tony was a potential master vampire who was wisely keeping his head down in Finney's territory; Gilly would not share this information with Finney however. Frankly, Gilly loathed Brian Finney and would have killed him if it were possible years ago, but Brian was as smart as he was tough, it was not a job Gilly was ready to take at present.

"I am going to lure the fledgling and his little helpers to the old college stadium and slaughter them all in one giant swoop. I want your men to hem them in once they are inside. You kill them if they try to escaped, however the fledgling and his black shadow are mine alone" Gilly said with authority.

"The old college stadium eh, good choice they have already walled up part and boarded up even more. It is a variable prison on the inside. When do you want to initiate your plan" Tony asked?

"Tomorrow night I will have them all there, so be prepared" Gilly answered.

Gilly got up and walked out of the bar without another word. When he was gone and the scouts returned; the band sat and had a drink together.

"We need to go up to the stadium tonight and put together a game plan of our own. I don't want any of us getting killed because we didn't know what we were doing and I am not for trusting Gilly at all, we are just guards and expendable. He admitted that we are facing a dangerous foe freely; that is unlike Gilly. Our prey is likely as dangerous as we are, so I want the advantage of home court and surprise on our side" Tony explained.

Tony's band of vampires finished their drinks and left for the stadium.

(At the Paradice club, 1030PM)

Jax was tending bar and holding court in her sweat way. It did not matter male or female patron they all loved Jax equally. It was not just her stellar body and movie starlet face, it was her sassy personality. Jax was also the best drink maker in town and she made you feel like you were her only customer in the club when she served you. Tonight Jazon hired new security for the club. All monsters, two dark skinned trolls and four werewolves. Enoch was in command of them. There were a few low level vampires in the club and Jazon spoke with each of them and warned them not to hunt in his club or he would hunt them down and kill them. They took it in stride and assured him they just wanted to dance and drink nothing more. Club Paradice was the most hopping club in the zip code.

"Watch the door" Enoch told the troll as he walked toward Jazon.

"Got it chief" The troll answered.

A bald headed vampire reached over the counter and grabbed Jax and pinned her to the other side of the counter.

"I am going to rape you and then drink your blood through your wounds" The vampire said.

"No your not love" Pegi said as her razor sharp knife tightened up to his throat suddenly. "Remove your hand or I will remove your head; your choice".

The vampire could smell the garlic on the knife blade. He was about to jerk back when he noticed out of the corner of his eyes Enoch and Jazon looking right at him. He let go of Jax and stepped back slowly.

"I will taste you in many ways before you die and you will whore for me" The vampire said.

Pegi kneed the vampire in the nuts and cut his face with the knife and stepped back out of his rang and pulled her pistol in one fluid movement. The vampire choked for a moment in pain and then stood up and pointed at Pegi.

"Anytime you feel able insect, try me" Pegi said flatly.

"Tell your boyfriend I will be waiting for him tomorrow night in the old college stadium, if he does not want you killed he better come and take care of me" Gilly said.

The bald assassin turned and walked out of the club and ran like hell once he was clear of the door. He was actually scared stupid he would not get away from Jazon in time and those damned wolves could track him down if he doesn't hurry.

Meanwhile back in the club Pegi was now behind the bar with Jax who was crying. Jazon was outside and so were Enoch and another big werewolf.

"Can he take you in wolf form Enoch" Jazon asked without looking at the giant wolfman?

"No" Enoch answered.

"Then hunt him" Jazon said in the form of an order not mean to be so pushy.

The other werewolf started to say something bitchy to Jazon but Enoch snarled low at him and he shut his trap until Jazon went back inside.

"If I wanted to do a blood suckers dirty work, I could work for Finney" The wolf said!

SHANE

"He is not them, he is us. Jazon is our leader and if he says hunt we hunt. He feeds us, protects us and treats us like men not beasts, with respect. If it were not for his girl's tears, he would be running the city instead of us. More, he made sure we were not at risk before sending us out to seek his enemy. Jazon is one of us and we owe him if not loyalty; then respect and friendship. I am going to hunt, you can stay here a cry in you dog dish boy" Enoch roared at the younger Werewolf!

Both men transformed and ran off into the night as huge silent werewolves. Nobody witnessed it and even if they did who in God's name would believe them.

Jazon called Ajay on his cell phone and told him what was going on. Ajay had just gotten home from a afternoon game and was dead tired until he heard what Jazon said and then he reached for his special shotgun with Pegi's loads in it.

"I am coming to stay in the hotel tonight with Silky to make sure they don't get us in our sleep, tomorrow we can deal these fools a bad hand if you feel me little brother" Ajay said in a rough tired voice.

"I feel you brother, I feel you. Be safe, and get rollin as soon as you can" Jazon said before he hung up.

Jazon walked over to Jax and Pegi, he jumped the bar without touching it at all. He landed like a panther on the other side next to Jax. Pegi was holding the still

SHANE

sobbing Jax; she let Jax go into Jazon's arms. Jazon leaned forward and kissed Pegi on the cheek.

"You saved Jax from getting abused" Jazon said.

Pegi noticed he did not say raped or killed.

"It is a trap no doubt" Pegi said.

"No doubt about it" Jazon answered. "I need you to fortify the hotel and structure the security for maximum effect, have Tad help you; he is very wise but a little to small and soft spoken to lead a defense effort it think, where you are not to soft in mind of attitude".

Pegi digested Jazon's words carefully and did not reply. Jazon had another bartender take over and then he swept the room and instructed the trolls to throw anyone out that starts anything but no killing, the werewolves were to protect all the girls working there and watch to make sure there was not abductions. They were more than up to the challenge and the crowds were already afraid of the giant men.

Pegi got into Jazon car and held Jax who was still trembling. Jazon got in and hit the key, the motor roared to life and he slapped in into 2nd and tapped the gas. The Mustang jumped into the street at 60mph and began to pick up speed fast. Jazon was mad but calm at the same time. Gilly had made a critical mistake, Brian Finney may own the city but that was only

because Jazon had not killed him yet. Now the game was on and Jazon was going to kill everyone involved.

(AT THE STADIUM)

Tony and his vampire posse were looking over the area for ambush spots and places to put false wall to trap the prey in with Gilly, but Tony was sure that Gilly did not want to meet the prey in a one on one fight; if he did the fledgling would be dead or Gilly would be. Therefore, Tony was hard at work figuring out how to kill the foe and not get himself or his men killed in the process, the hell with Gilly. Finally Tony found that the training room was a perfect place to ambush the prey and be safe themselves. Tony's men rebuilt the area to serve their needs and design. It was morning before they were done; they were no surprised or put off. Tony had a habit of traveling prepared. All of his crew's weapons and blood supply were brought along when they came to check out the stadium. They settled in laundry room and took turns resting until the battle to come later that night.

(At Gilly's home)

The bald assassin barely escaped the werewolves. He jumped in the river and swam for miles under the water and came out at Camas and ran back to Portland across the Lynn Jackson Bridge. He was well dried when he reach his home and happy to have eluded his followers. Gilly went and took a warm shower and had some fruit. Yes fruit. Gilly was odd in many ways but as a sailor he was in the habit of eating fresh fruit as all sailors were to keep scurvy away. It was impossible for Gilly to get scurvy but no matter he enjoyed the taste. Fruit had the added benefit of giving him a pleasant breath which hid what he really was.

"You have set this up well Gilly my boy" The bald vampire said to himself.

Gilly called a lady friend that worked nights and invited her over for morning sex and she agreed to come over because Gilly was very good at making her loose her breath in the throws of passion. She arrived thirty minute later and Gilly pleasured her for two hours none stop and then they both slept well and deeply, her from exhaustion, Gilly from contentment.

If Gilly was not so arrogant and self assured he would have been wise to make damn sure Tony had the stadium all locked up and ready, but Gilly had never lost before, so he was not worried and he should have been, Jazon did not intend to let anyone live now. Quite simply put Jazon was on the war path and out for scalp.

SHANE

(AT THE HOTEL FOR THE MAGICAL FOLK).

Ajay and Jazon were eating breakfast with Pegi and Enoch. Enoch was explaining what happened the night before. He and the other wolf with him had run the vampire to ground and cornered him in an industrial park near the river when the vampire jumped in the water and was gone. Jazon listened without saying anything. Enoch began to apologize when his young wolf partner came in.

"Why the hell are you apologizing to him, it is not like he could have done any better, filthy blood sucker" The young wolf yelled.

In an instant Enoch was on his feet and changing. He would have killed the pup in anger this time. However Pegi took over. She laid the fool low with a rolling pin to the head; Enoch's giant snarling head turned and looked at Pegi, she gave him a hard look, he calmed down and lost his fur once again to be the man.

"I will not have blood all over my kitchen and that is final" Pegi said "Besides that little jackass had that coming for a while. Honestly Enoch why do you put up with that kids, what a dickhead"?

"I look after him because he is so young and if I don't his stupidity will land him in the soup. He is strong and fierce and willing but green to the gills as a person. He must learn to extend his hand in friendship as well as combat, but I don't; even I am sick of his shit" Enoch answered.

"Never mind Terry, he will make it to adulthood if he learns his place in the pack and respect for our friends. We have to get this assassin before he gets us one by one and he wants to kill Jazon first because he is the strongest among all of us, then he will take down Ajay to spite us; although he is not among the most powerful. No disrespect Ajay" Wolf said.

"None taken man, I am not the man; I know that but I won't lay down either, he is going to have to put me on my back hard if he wants me dead" Ajay said with a wild look on his face.

"You all don't know what my brother is made of, I do. I witnessed it first hand against an entire family of vampires, he took down more than I did and he got hurt so bad if Pegi was not near he would have died, yet he didn't stop or step back or call for help. He locked his jaw and went to work" Jazon said.

"It is all true, that young man has more heart than any human I have ever known, and the resolve to use it no matter the cost, it is a rare quality and usually fatal. Heroes always die well" Pegi added.

The group sat there as the coffee and tea pot was sent around the huge table again. Wolf looked at Enoch

SHANE

and they were wordlessly discussing something. What was it with Wolf anyway? Wolf seemed a human but everyone respected and loved him, and his shadow Biz was a total mystery as well. Biz seemed a normal teenager who was exceptionally quiet. Wolf warned Ajay once not to approach Biz aware, but he did not elaborate at all and block attempts to get a more comprehensive explanation.

Tad came in and was lifted onto the table by a faerie. He had a small chair and table set that was put on the table during meals so he could converse with everyone at eye level. This morning he went with just the chair.

"I have been working with some of our hidden brethren to make sure you're not going to get jumped at the stadium, well it is not deserted up there. There are at the least five men in that place that went in and never came out. To the best of the field Brownies knowledge there is not larger predators or killer monsters in that place, just mice or coons" Tad explained.

"Ambush" Enoch said?

"Ambush" Wolf said.

"Then we are going in first to make sure it is not a death trap" Enoch said.

"No".

"What" Enoch asked?

SHANE

"No, you are not going Enoch, I need your strong arms and hard head here looking after things with Pegi. I will take Terry in your place, you said he can fight well" Jazon said.

"Well... yes that kid in a real monster in a melee, but he is young and won't obey" Enoch said.

"I will take him nonetheless. Ajay load your shotgun, two pistols, carry you knives; you're with me and I will take Block the troll, we like each other and he can't be killed by anything I know of" Jazon explained.

Ajay smiled, he liked the big troll, strong and thoughtful. Ajay was happy to have that guy at his back, Jazon was good, but Block could not be killed at all, that made him a good back guard for the adventuring human.

"I think that is not a good idea, what if your killed" Wolf asked?

"Block will return our broken bodies then" Ajay said all flip.

"You would not say that if Silky was here to whup your ass for it" Enoch and Tad said in unison.

"Even if she was here, you think I am going to let my boy go alone, that is not happening. I would rather die standing up like a man then live on my knees

SHANE

VAMPIRE HERO SAGA

SHANE

CHAPTER 10: GILLY'S FOLLY

I am not sure why but Gilly was not paying close attention to the fact his opponent was likely the most dangerous foe he has ever faced. Moreover, Gilly made Jazon so insane with anger that the new vampire hunter was going to thoroughly destroy him and everyone involved with Gilly. Gilly seemed like he was playing a game with friends, not a deadly enemy. Jazon would remind him that very night.

(Dusk 7:32PM)

Tony and his six vampire cohorts were ready with crossbows in hand and poison garlic arrows on hand. They had the false walls up and reinforced with steel rebar so they would not come down if hit. They would not stop a vampire but they would slow them up so they could receive an arrow or two. Even after all of his efforts he still did not feel ready for some reason. His men had spread out and poured bleach all over the place to kill the prey's sense of smell and place small strobe lights to mess up the vampire fledglings night vision. Tony had survived and lost very few men because he was careful not to take stupid chances with any of their lives. Still Tony was uneasy.

SHANE

(8:05 at the Hotel for magical folks)

"The sun is down boys, you ready" Ajay asked.

Block winked at Ajay and grabbed his solid steel war hammer that weight 80lbs. It was reputed to be the hammer of Thor, but who knows if that is even possible. Terry was less than impressed at first about being assigned to go with the group until Jazon told him that he needed the young werewolf's mighty battle skills to live to see another day. Once Terry's pride was stroked he was actually raring to go.

"How about you Jazon, ready to roll baby" Ajay asked?

Jazon sat on a stool sharpening his sword and two daggers. He turned and looked at Ajay and the other two and all three were startled by the face they saw. Jazon was not angry, he was miles past angry, his eyes were almost yellow and the insides were turbulent and moving like a tempest. Jazon shook his head that he was ready.

"Fine let's go" Ajay said.

"Wait a tick boy" Tad yelled at him as he came into the room dragging something heavy behind him. Despite Tad's small stature he was as strong as or stronger than a normal sized human man.

"What you got there Tad" Jazon asked suddenly?

SHANE

"Ring-mail the finest I have ever made. It is for Ajay. It will not allow teeth or claws, arrows, daggers or bladed weapons to penetrate it. Bullets might; but then again it is enchanted so likely even bullets would not go through" Tad said with a huge smile.

"It looked to heavy to be worn by a human, even one as strong and conditioned as Ajay" Block said.

"No it is not heavy, it is just cumbersome to carry with these small arms so I dragged it in here" Tad said as he flipped the mail like a sheet towards Ajay.

Ajay reached out and grabbed it. It was as lite as a babies kiss and soft as well. However, it was a fine armor. Jazon stabbed it with his dagger and it did not go through, and he smile and gave Tad a fist tap. Ajay pulled off his Kevlar vest and shirt; he slid the Mythical Silver ring-mail over his head and on to his body. It was nearly weightless and it shimmered like a diamond.

"Now I believe we are all read to leave" Block said.

They left Jazon and Ajay's hotrods in the parking lot and took an old dump truck with a brand new motor and tranny. Ajay had it super charged for just such an occasion. Block climbed in the back and so did Ajay and Jazon, they had Terry drive the truck just incase it was spotted they would think the kid was just out joy riding. Terry knew the way and set off for the stadium.

(9:03PM)

SHANE

Gilly was in route to the stadium feeling pretty cocky. The way he had lured Jazon into a fight not of his own choosing; would make all the difference in the out come. Gilly had his mini crossbow with poison darts and three water balloons filled with holy water. Gill hated guns; however he loved blades and carried a lot of them. He had his big Bowie knife on his belt in plain sight. He was strutting and whistling a happy tune as he got within plain sight of the old stadium. Gilly could smell the bleach and knew that Tony had been worth the money, Gilly approved of the measure, Gilly also saw the miniature lights all over the place and understood their use as well. Yes, Gilly would have to re-evaluate Tony's worth to him.

"Hello Gilly" Tony said from a shadow that gilly just walked by.

Gilly spun and pulled his blade in one motion.

"I could have killed you right where you stand" Gilly snarled!

Tony walked out of the shadows with his crossbow leveled at Gilly's heart and two more vampires came out of the shadows behind him. Damn Gilly was caught completely unaware.

"I think not Gilly, you would have never lived long enough if you came looking for trouble" Tony said in a conversational tone. "We have everything ready for your little surprise party tonight, come I will show you".

Gilly smiled but was mad at being caught, some with Tony but mostly with himself. Tony's preparations were much better than Gilly expected, the fledgling was hosed once he entered the trap. Gilly was really starting to like Tony. Gilly's first assessment of him was low level thug leader, now he knew this to be false in everyway. Tony was a formidable enemy or ally depending on where you stand, and Gilly was standing as the employer so he was pretty happy with how it was going his way at present.

"The false walls are made to slam shut and send the prey into a maze where my men could injure or kill them, except the fledgling who is all yours once you point him out for us, the shadow is a black man so we know which he will be" Tony explained the set up as they walked.

Gilly was plenty interested in the how he was going to set up the Fledgling for the kill, Tony's men were not mere thugs either, but finely tunes warriors with good technical know how to build and spring complex traps.

(9:23pm).

Terry was feeling his fortune was rising in the world, Enoch let him go as the sole representative of the werewolf pack. Jazon who was the leader of all the free magical creatures hand picked him for his battle ability and ferocity, Ajay had shook his hand and welcomed him and told him I trust you, don't die on me. Block the old powerful immortal troll took him a side and said to use speed against a stronger opponent and strength a faster one, but use your head to know which it is you face, because you head is your best weapon. Terry was pleased that Block who was an elder talked to him at all, it was a high honor to be addressed by one and in private to boot; good stuff.

The road leading to the old stadium was ever so slightly twisted and down hill in the midway point. It was just after that point when Terry's werewolf senses picked up bleach.

"Oh snap, they are trying to screw us up by pouring bleach all over the place, it might work on a vampire but not me, there are several distinct smells coming from that place, at the least five attackers maybe more" Terry whispered knowing Jazon could hear it clear as a bell.

"I can smell them as well, the bleach is a clever tactic against natural vampires, I will use that someday to our advantage. What else do you see and think or smell Terry" Jazon asked?

Terry was floored at the amount of responsibility and trust they were showing him. He could hear Jazon explaining what Terry had told him and what he thought they should do. Suddenly, Jazon said stop the truck. Terry heard him and felt no heard the massive weight of Block leave the dump truck bed and fade into the dark. Block was a troll and in the dark not even a vampire could see him unless he was moving and Block moved fast for a huge creature carrying an 80lbs hammer.

"Go up the back of the Stadium and get out and let them see you do it Terry, walk around the truck and look underneath it, be on guard they will be watching you" Jazon said.

Terry drove around to the loading docks in the back of the stadium, but not close enough to have anyone shoot or jump him and his senses missed nothing. There were indeed two people watching him, both vampires by the smell.

(10PM)

Jazon grabbed Ajay and jumped up about twenty feet into the air and let the truck go out from under them. Ajay was about to tense and be afraid but it happened so fast and he was already on the ground softly with Jazon pulling him into the field. They walked about seventy-five yards when Jazon stopped and then whistled softly. A brownie popped up out of nowhere.

SHANE

"Hey gov, how can I help you" The brownie asked?

"Hello little cousin, I need to know if the trash in the stadium put anything like land mines or traps in the field leading up to the building itself" Jazon asked?

"Naw, they're too stupid for that. We did check all of the field to make sure though at Tad's request, he must have though they want you dead pretty bad to mine an old field. If they had we would have disarmed or moved them where they would step on them outside of our field" The brownie explained.

"Great little cousin you have been a tremendous help to us; now go somewhere safe for awhile and let us hunt this trash down and put them on their backs for good with dimes in their eyes" Jazon said.

"I heard that brother" Ajay added.

The browning disappeared into the field and Jazon lead Ajay silently through the field. Jazon was amazed how well his friend had adapted to this crazy life. More, for a big guy he was quiet even by vampire standards and he was a human still. There was a light on inside the second floor area and one in the basement level. Jazon looked at both lights and then at Ajay and held out a hand palm down. Ajay understood this was a question, so he reached out and put his hand over the top of Jazon's hand. Jazon smiled and they went on into the structure and the adventure of the night.

SHANE

(10:12PM)

Gilly was watching Terry through a window; the kid really was a good actor and was selling mechanical problems with the truck. Gilly made sure that nobody approached the boy; or they might give away the game. Tony was insulted by this comment. Terry knew they were watching him, what Terry did not know was that Jazon and Ajay were long gone and he was alone or werewolf or not he would have been less confident and cavalier.

"Who the hell is the kid in the big truck, why is he here, is this part of the plan" Gilly hissed at Tony?

"Some random kid in a truck joy riding does not mean anything and since our plans are set up in the stadium and not the grounds, the kid is not an issue" Tony stated in an irate tone.

Gill looked at the wily vampire and knew Tony was not to be pushed lightly and never when he had his well trained crew backing him up. Gilly had made a serious mistake when he thought this group were common thugs, they were all seasoned MERCS. Tony spoke an order and a single vampire went out side to kill the kid and get ride of him. Tony led Gilly and the others away in preparation for Jazon's arrival. They should have waited and watched, but they didn't.

SHANE

The vampire slipped up quietly behind Terry and pulled a stiletto out of his sleeve, he closed the distance to Terry lightning fast and was about to deliver the blade to Terry's heart when Terry turned and smiled at him.

"Naughty, naughty trying to stab a kid in the back what bad manners you have" Terry teased him.

The vampire lunged at Terry and to his complete surprise; the kid did not move in anyway, he let the blade go right into his chest.

"Is that all you go man" Terry asked?

Terry back handed the vampire into the truck bed and transformed into a full werewolf smiling the entire time. He advanced on the Vampire with the stiletto he pulled from his own chest and rammed it into the vampire's eye and racked his body with his steel claws across his rib cage. The vampire tried to flee but he was so totally taken off guard that Terry tore him apart. The young werewolf ripped off the vampires arms and threw them into the back of the truck. The vampire kicked Terry in the nuts, and Terry staggered but regained he composer instantly, he was going the finish the vampire, but now he was mad so he really made the blood drinker pay for that misdeed. The vampires head and heart were rent form his body and Terry was soaked in blood and he decided it was time to raise some hell so the Jazon and Ajay who were still in the truck could sneak into the building. Terry went and looked in the back of the truck and there was only the two vampire arms laying there.

"Well, I'll be damned" Terry chuckled.

He decided he was not early for the dance; rather he was late. Therefore Terry went back to his plan to raise some hell, might as well.

(10:27PM)

Jazon grabbed Ajay around the waist and Jumped four flights of stair straight up. Ajay was getting used to just holding still and letting Jazon do his amazing moves as he saw fit. Boy could he use Jazon on his football team, they would never loose another game with him playing defense. And who could stop him on offense. Ajay did not voice his thoughts because they were not alone. Jazon grabbed the rail and hauled him and Ajay over and set them on the floor silently and he pointed at the far wall and made a cup with his hands and indicated the space inside his of hands and then looked at the walls. Ajay was not sure, so he pointed at his head and made a blowing face, meaning air head. Suddenly Ajay got it the walls were hollow and fake, they had entered the trap set for them. Jazon was warning Ajay.

"Let's see what they have for us shall we" Jazon spoke out loud?

SHANE

"Works for me" Ajay said as he pumped a shell into his shotgun and dropped the safety.

There were two vampires watching them on the other side of the wall, Jazon kicked the wall and it blew in. The vampires used their pre-arranged escape route and were gone before the dust from the wall falling was gone.

"They went through there" Jazon said.

Ajay followed Jazon through a small hole in the wall that was not a natural part of the building design. Jazon move fast but Ajay stayed with him at some cost in effort. Just as Jazon jump out of the hole; a log full of sharp ruff spikes dropped where he was standing, before Jazon knew what happened; Ajay grabbed him and yanked him back out of the way.

"Damn boy be careful I don't want to do this alone; I am not good enough and I am not brave enough without you either" Ajay told him in haste.

Jazon drop kicked the log and it slammed and stuck in the opposite wall. Ajay tapped Jazon on the shoulder pushed passed him. Ajay looked around the room and hallway for traps, wires or anything that looked like a don't go there sign. He could not find anything that looked wrong.

"Smell anything Jazon, or hear anything. They are after all hosting this party" Ajay said.

Jazon looked at Ajay and they both burst out laughing.

(10:53PM)

The sound of laughter came drifting eerily to where Gilly was. He wrongly mistook it for the cries of agony and was delighted. It was only Tony that kept him from running down there to see for himself. Tony was beginning to think Gilly's reputation was not well earned; the man seemed too stupid to live as long as he had. However, Tony was no fool and Gilly was likely acting dumb to keep him off guard. Tony thought after we deal with the hunters, we better kill Gilly as well.

(CRASH)!

An entire wall exploded into the training room, a concrete one, not the false wood walls and a huge dark creature came like a rampaging Rhino through.

"What, am I disturbing your ladies" Block yelled as he charged.

The Troll took fifteen arrows to his body, they did not even penetrate his out hide properly and he loved garlic and holy water so it was a refreshing sensation

SHANE

to him. The vampires realize it was hopeless and Tony hollered.

"Run for it if you want to live, we will regroup in the area" Tony screamed.

The troll was fast as he was big and powerful and he Rhinoed right through all the traps Tony set and busted the walls with his hammer as he ran. Block kept the vampire running as fast as they could just to stay out of his reach.

On the other side of the stadium Terry was all wolfed up and running down one of the entry tunnels to the playing field.

(11:09pm).

Jazon came ripping out of a hall way and could see the fleeing vampires, so he took another hallway to cut them off. He hoped that Block would run them right into him and Ajay, so they could cut them down like they did on the swamp island. That did not happen. Jazon and Ajay ran right into stairs.

"Go down the damn stair, block is herding them to the field so we can fight in the open" Ajay yelled as he jumped the rail and fell eight feet down to the landing and then ran for the next stairs!

SHANE

"Right" Jazon said and he jumped down to and followed his best friend.

(In the hallway that lead to the playing field)

The vampires knew that all their plans were in the soup now. All most of them could think of was survival. They ran as fast as they could and that damn monster was keeping up somehow. What was that thing anyway?

"We will regroup and the field where we can spread out and fight as a team, it is too small in here to press that advantage" Tony yelled.

The vampires made the field first and could see a shadow coming fast up the tunnel across the field. Tony pointed to set of vampire and the tunnel and they ran over and set up a cross fire behind some barrels and other junk dumped on the field.

Jazon and Ajay were on the second floor balcony and saw Terry about to come out of a tunnel into a crossbow ambush.

"OMG, their going to kill him and we are too far away.

It happened so fast it scared Ajay. Jazon changed, his eyes went clear as glass, his ears were pointed and his teeth were long and sharp. But it was his hands that drew the most attention. Where the ends of

Jazon's fingers had been; were now what looked like golden metal claws.

(SNARL)

Terry came ripping out of the tunnel saw Gilly and Tony and accelerated to get them. He did not see the two vampires hiding in the barrels and other industrial building materials stacked around. The football field looked more like a building zone that a sports field, way too much stuff on it. Terry was smiling until the two vampires jumped up and fired crossbow bolts at him. It was too late to get out of the way, he was going to take a shaft to the heart and one to the head, his life was over because he did not listen to the lessons Enoch had tried repeatedly to teach him. Damn it all he never even got to say he was sorry for all the shit he caused and how much he appreciated Enoch as a mentor and only friend.

(ROAR)!

Terry was knocked to the ground by someone so fast and hard that he made a forward crater in the ground. Terry looked up and Jazon was standing over him with the arrows in his chest and the points

SHANE

sticking out his back. Jazon did not speak he just looked down and winked and then he went after the Vampires.

The two vampires closest to the exit turned to leave and found it blocked by Block. They stopped and ran for the next tunnel; and when the disappeared Block scream in anger.

(Blam, racket, Bam).

Ajay walked out of the tunnel with two heads in his right hand. Ajay had literally blown the vampires heads off and since he used Pegi's special rounds the vampires were dead, they can regenerate with the loads in their bodies. Ajay tossed the heads at Tony and then stood his ground in the opening shotgun and pistol at the ready.

"Kill them" Tony ordered!

Four arrows his Ajay and knocked him flat. Only the one aimed at his leg got him; the others bounce of his mail shirt. Still Ajay was down, a vampire got close enough to stab him; Ajay pulled the trigger and his shotgun belched and the vampire exploded.

Gilly tossed what looked like a grenade at Block, when it exploded the gas made the giant troll sleepy;

no matter how hard Block tried he could not keep standing. The troll finally passed out and fell flat on the ground with a loud thump. Gilly was not finished; he pulled two silver throwing knives out and sank them into Terry's back when the werewolf was getting up. Terry was on the ground wreathing in pain with the knives burning into his body. Silver is poisonous to Werewolves.

Jazon was the only one left on his feet, and he had three more crossbow bolts in his chest. Jazon pulled them out and stood if front of Terry so they could not hurt him anymore, but he could not attack either.

"I am going to kill all of you, well all but that thing over there that seems to be unkillable, but it will hurt it that I killed all of you while he slept" Gilly said.

"Don't bet on it you bald headed bitch" Ajay yelled!

Gilly pulled another knife and through it at Ajay, it hit the black man in the hip and went in to the hilt just below the mail. Gilly must have known by the way he tossed the knife and where. Ajay was in great pain with tears in his eyes, but he pulled the knife out and slid it into his belt and got up as blood rush out of his two leg wounds. Ajay looked at his little brother and best friend and was sure they were about to die, or at the least he was. Ajay ratcheted another shell into his shotgun and pointed it right at Gilly.

"Go on toss some more shit my way I dare you" Ajay said in a harsh tone.

Gilly was impressed; but Tony was not pleased, he saw what that gun did to three of his crew, if he got hit with that thing he was finished. That would never be a problem, Gilly tossed another gas grenade at Ajay's feet, Ajay kicked it away but it was too late and he had lost a lot of blood. Jazon watched at his boy fell flat on his face out cold.

Jazon pulled the knives out of Terry's back and tossed them in the stands, but the damage was done; Terry was too ill to fight anymore, and damn it Jazon brought him here, If the kid died Jazon would make sure it was not alone. Even worse still Ajay he brother, best friend and the strongest, bravest man he ever knew is going to die as well. Jazon was not going to die until he killed all of the rest of these trash and Brian Finney, after that he no longer cared.

The four remaining Vampires pointed their crossbows at Ajay not Jazon, they were about to fire when a huge werewolf came out of the dark tunnel and snarled like a lion roaring. It stood over Ajay and growled. The two remaining members leveled their crossbows at the Werewolf and a smaller figure walked out and looked at them. Jazon said one word.

"Biz"?

The boy looked at the vampires and they shot at him. Biz raised his hand and the arrows burst into flames. Biz stepped forward and flame engulf him as he walked, Biz's body shimmered and where biz used to be was now Bizerc the demon of fire.

"You would slay my human host, minor insects that you are; I still feel compelled to erase your stain form the world as a reminder not to ever attack my host" The demon said.

Flames shot out of the demon's mouth and the two offending vampires were turned to ash. The huge wolf howled and Bizerc looked at him and nodded. The werewolf had a tattoo of the moon in ¾ set on his arm Jazon noticed, as he lifted Ajay off the ground and jumped into the stands and off into the night. Bizerc walked with his huge wings folded over to Block and lifted the troll easily over his shoulder; hammer and all. Bizerc continued on over and picked Terry up off the ground. The demon turned to Jazon and spoke.

"Jazon Wild you are the best among men and creatures, you know my secret now and Biz's. You have to decided what you want to do with that knowledge, but I will give but a single command out of comradeship" Bizerc said as he looked directly at Tony and Gilly. "Kill them".

"I will" Jazon promised.

SHANE

The big red and gold demon took the sleeping warriors away into the night. However, werewolves circled the area in the dark and both the vampires and Jazon saw them. Tony looked at Gilly.

"Your screwed man; and I did not sign on for this shit. You're on your own babe" Tony said.

The wily vampire tossed a handful of homemade grenades that were filled with purple smoke and a stronger soporific to confuse the werewolves enough for Tony to escape. The stand and area was full of these and in the purple haze Tony slipped away and ran for his life. He made it all the way out side the stadium and was half way across the field when two brownies shoe stringed him and he went face down. When he jumped up he was looking into the eyes of the last man he wanted to see.

"I can't let you go this time Tony you attacked my clan, and they would not allow a leader who let's their enemies go" The man said.

"Hey, I didn't know these were your wolf pace. Come on for old time sake, we were best mates once along time ago" Tony said.

"True, but you got in bed with that nutter Gilly and he has spent your life for you because of it. No worries about him though, Jazon is going to rip his apart" The man said.

SHANE

Tony stepped back as the man shimmered and instantly became the biggest werewolf who ever lived. The wolf snapped his mighty jaws together once and Tony's head was gone and the wolf's claws ripped the heart and body apart.

"Hey don't be leave in trash in me field fuzzy wuzzy, or I will come and take a crap on your pillow while you sleep" The brownie hollered!

(HOOOOOWL with laughter).

The big werewolf laughed deeply and cleaned up what was left of Tony's destroyed body and walked away.

(1200AM)

Face to face across the tore up field Jazon and Gilly stood looking at each other. Gilly noticed that his arrows did nothing to Jazon but make him angry, so he tossed his crossbow away and his darts and grenades. Gilly pulled out his Bowie knife and dagger and showed them to Jazon.

"Let us settle this with blades like the gentlemen of old. No more tricks fledgling, just plain open combat

SHANE

winner take all. And by winner I mean who ever is still alive" Gilly said with a smile.

"Jazon".

"What"?

"My name is Jazon Wild; and I except your terms Gilly".

Gilly smiled and then bowed low. He walked up to Jazon and put his knife back in the sheath. He extended his open hand. Jazon shook it even though he thought it was a trick.

"I told you no more trick or bullshit, I wanted to shake your hand. You have in a short time become more powerful than I have in my many centuries, and you have a strong army of fearless friends at you back if you fall. I have no one and until this moment I thought is was right in my life style. I can see now I was so completely in error, but it is too late now to change that. One final thing before we kill each other. I would never have harmed the girl, it is below me to harm a helpless child, I am a warrior and an assassin, but I have a code that I live by and mindless brutality against one like her especially with her beauty is repulsive to me" Gill explained.

"I believe you Gilly, but you are way too good for me not to kill you now. I might be able to survive your traps, but obviously my friends are not so lucky. If you did not work for Brian Finney I would let you walk out of here if you gave me your word to leave and never

SHANE

return, but we know that can't happen. You have been a dangerous foe, not a pleasure, but a definite challenge" Jazon said.

The two warriors let go of each others hand after a brief hard last grip and a mutual smile and they backed up about ten feet apart. Gilly pulled his Bowie knife back out and took a fighting stance. Jazon tossed his coat off, what was left of it. He pulled his sword from between his shoulders and Gilly's face sunk because Jazon had a serious advantage with the sword in bladed combat. Jazon laid the sword down behind him and then reach behind his back with both hands and pulled twin long curved daggers out. Gilly saw the beautiful blades and was envious.

"A gift from a gnome armor maker, so is the sword, they are unbreakable and never loose their edge. If you beat me Gilly it would please me that you take them and use them to kill Brian Finney someday" Jazon said.

"I accept, if I win, I will plan Finney's demise for I hate him as well as you do" Gilly said.

Jazon nodded and they began to circle looking for an opening. The problem was they were both very skilled fighters. Gilly was a long time pirate and assassin, Jazon was an expert in Kajukenbo a Gungfu combine martial art, and knife fighting. They finally clashed and sparks flew from the blades. To an observer it looked like two open bladed blenders going at each other. There was a small hurricane coming off the blades as they moves and dust flew every where, but did not slow either man down. Jazon could see that he was far faster than Gilly and knew he could kill him at anytime, he decided to show this man so respect and let his last combat be a valiant one.

"Oh shit, I am in way over my head here" Gilly chuckled as he stopped fighting. "Okay I know how this is going to end so let me tell you something and also ask you something to boot"?

"Okay, go ahead" Jason answered as he stepped by to give Gilly some room and peace of mind.

Gilly liked this man; damn it why didn't they meet before he took the contract, Gilly could have had a new fresh life. Oh well.

"First, Brian Finney is not as fast as you, not even close, but he is a far superior swordsman so be careful not to get sucked into a sword duel with him, in close you would kill him, but at the tip of his Rapier you may die. Now the request, I want you to bury my Bowie knife in that little bastard Mark O"Day's chest up the hilt" Gilly snarled.

To Gilly's horror Jazon sat down and laughed. He looked up at Gilly and gestured to relax a minute. Jazon took second to restrain himself.

"It was Mark who turned me Gilly, I hate him and I will gladly pin him with your knife with a glad heart" Jazon said with a mean smile. "Shall we finish this up before the sun comes up, I am immune but you are not".

"Right, very generous of you to think of a fair playing field" Gilly said.

Gilly fought with a new vigor, he was a mad man; he threw caution to the wind and pursued Jazon like rabid animal. Jazon got stabbed several times and so did Gilly. Their blades were amazing as the dance of death went on the brownies who watched had never seen a display of skill and ferocity to match this before. It was both horrible and wonderful at the same time. Later the brownies would retell the story over nutmeg tea to Tad and others for the next century.

Gilly finally reached his limit and he made a misstep, Jazon impaled him through the heart, and broke the arm holding the Bowie knife in one deft move. Gilly knew this was it so he tossed his other weapon in the grass. Blood was dripping out his mouth and he coughed; however Gilly was smiling.

"Go get your sword son and finish me quickly please. I have had enough, you paid my a great deal of respect and honor already, just allow me a quick clean death" Gilly cough as blood foamed on his lips.

Jazon walked over to his sword and picked it up and walked back to Gilly who was on his knees looking up. Jazon took a knee in front of Gilly who was in a hell of a lot a pain.

"It is a shame that we met like this, you would have made a fine teacher to the younger ones, who need discipline and guidance. Your combat skills are truly amazing, I am not happy about the end for you, I take no pleasure in this, but I will make sure Finney and Mark both pay for your death, my word on it. One last thing, I am going to give you a king's burial at sea Gilly as is your right" Jazon said.

Gilly just looked at Jazon with the first tears in his eyes of over two centuries, he let them fall on his chest and mingle with his blood. Why had he not met this man before that bastard Finney made him go after him.

"Goodbye my new and only friend" Gilly said.

In a lightning fast movement it was over, Jazon did not even get any blood on his sword when he beheaded Gilly. Jazon was about remove Gilly's heart and then decided not to. He pulled his dagger out of Gilly's chest and cleaned it on his pant leg. Jazon looked around and found a cloth tarp, he rolled Gilly up in it and tied it shut and picked up Gilly's weapons and Gilly's body and went home.

VAMPIRE HERO SAGA

SHANE

CHAPTER 11: GILLY'S REVENGE

When the sunset over the mouth of the Columbia River where it meets the sea Jazon and his entire clan were there to send Gilly off to a better life and the peace the man had never know.

(FIVE DAYS EARLIER).

The hotel was all abuzz when Jazon returned home. Pegi had her faerie helpers making herb medicines per her instructions and the lovely girls work tirelessly for Pegi as usual.

Jazon walked into the kitchen and opened the meat locker and put Gilly inside of hit on the floor. When Jazon came out; he tossed Gilly's bloody hardware on the counter; Pegi who suddenly gave him a dirty look and then smiled. Jazon looked terrible.

"Thanks for saving Ajay last night Enoch" Jazon grunted through a dry throat.

Pegi and Enoch looked at Jazon and then each other.

"I did not save Ajay last night, Biz did I was told" Enoch said.

SHANE

"No, he was saved by a huge werewolf, and you're the only one that big transformed" Jazon said.

Enoch looked down and swallowed hard.

"No, I am not the only one; he is even bigger than I am. He is the leader of our pack, I told him you should know but he had not given permission to inform you of his true identity" Enoch said.

"Well, I will deal with that later. I feel like shit and I have lost a lot of blood if I don't eat soon I am going to need Pegi to revive me as well. How is Ajay and Terry doing" Jazon asked?

(Up stairs in a private room).

Ajay woke up covered in bandages and herbs, he was in more pain than he could normally bear. He was hurt as usually really bad, he likely would have died if not for Pegi's magic hoodoo. An arm went across Ajay's vision and he saw a tattoo. Ajay's hand shot up and grabbed the arm and held it tightly in his powerful grip. Ajay saw the ¾ moon tattoo on the arm and followed it up to the owners face. Ajay was stunned for a moment but didn't say so.

"You have to keep my secret Ajay, I have come to your rescue twice now, and I have been a thorn in Finney's ass for years, if he learns my true identity I am a goner

SHANE

and so are the rest of my clan and the larger family. There are only a few of us strong enough to keep the wild wolf packs out of our territory. They will not enter my domain so long as I live, Enoch is my second but he is not my equal in size or strength, I am the true Alpha dog" The man said.

"I reluctantly give my word, but Jazon needs to know" Ajay said.

The door opened and the man pulled down his sleeves and left as Silky ran in crying. She jumped on the bed and lay on Ajay's chest.

"Idiot, you almost got killed again. I am not going to let you out of my sight if you don't start being more careful" Silky said sternly.

"We are at war girl, and I am not leaving my boy's back unguarded. I fell on my ass out there and could have gotten Jazon killed, Terry too. I got to get stronger or I am not going to be of any use to Jazon. He almost had to give up his life to save mine, I can never let that happen again" Ajay said solemnly.

The door opened and Jazon walked in still covered in blood and cut up with an arrow still in his back. He looked hungry, his eyes were pink tinged and he looked dry.

"I called Pat and told him I need a barrel of fresh blood asap, he is bringing it over. You look like shit amigo" Jazon said.

"Look who is talking man. Come here let me pull that damn shaft out of you back, it went in through your chest didn't it" Ajay asked/

"Yes, I broke the front off butt was too busy fighting to figure out how to get the rest out, Give it a yank" Jazon said.

Silky looked about to barf, her lovely tan skin was pale and her lips blue.

"What they hell is wrong with you too? You speak of death and pain and injuries like it is nothing, you are so injured, such terrible pain and misery yet you play it all off" Silky said with tears running down her face. "What kind of man can endure this, how stronger are you two really"?

Jazon looked at Ajay and sighed, he step forward shook his boys hand and turned kissed Silky on the cheek and left the room.

"Baby sit down and let me holler at you a minute" Ajay said.

Silky came and curled up next to him on the bed and looked into Ajay's caramel colored eyes, which used to be dark brown now they were lighter. Ajay was changing in inches into something more than he was.

"Silky, Jazon and I have been up to butts in trouble all our lives. My momma was a strong black woman and my pops was a quiet strong black man, Jazon never had any of that. His father was a bad man, beat that

SHANE

boy down, and he beat his mamma too. When Jazon was 13 years old he pulled a knife on his father and killed him for hurting his mother one too many times. Jazon himself almost died from blood loss, his father was an army ranger and could fight, but he made the mistake of teaching Jazon. The combination of the beatings and the training made Jazon stronger than his father ever knew and afraid of nothing. Jazon can endure great suffering and physical damage and he will not stop ever... until he wins, not even death frightens him. When we were kids, I got in a lot of fights. Once these jerks decided to gang up on me because none of them could beat me alone, they had me down and one of them pulled out a sharp piece of metal; he told me they were going to cut my face up so nobody ever crossed them again. My mom saw Jazon and said I was at the school playing ball. When Jazon showed up and saw my face bleeding..." Ajay explained.

"What happened baby, tell me what did he do" Silky probed as she ran her fingers over the scar on his cheek?

There were tears in his eyes as he recalled how close he came to death that day; and what he best friend did to the boys who hurt him.

"He grabbed the first one off me, the one with the metal. He took the metal away and stabbed him in the spine with it and as he was falling Jazon kneed him in the face so hard it broke his neck. He turned on the

SHANE

other two; he caught the Asian kid in the mouth a snap kick and broke his jaw, the third kids was not so lucky. Jazon grabbed him by the throat and broke his nose with his own forehead, he kneed him in the nuts, broke his arm and his neck. Jazon tossed him aside and went back after the Asian kid who produced a knife and cut Jazon's neck. He nicked an artery they say, because there was blood everywhere. Jazon did not even notice, he knocked the knife out of his hand and choke slammed the kid head first in to the concrete giving him brain damage. He scooped me up and carried me home as he bleed to death. I will never forget my mother's face when she open the door and Jazon stood there with his throat cut and both me and him covers in blood. My dad came out and took me out of Jazon's arms. Jazon went and sat on the curb dying, but would not enter my mamma's perfect clean home because of all the blood. When the cops and the ambulance showed up they found Jazon sitting in shock rocking back and forth. The police pulled guns on him and ordered him to lay on the ground, he did not know they existed, he was to far gone. My father ran outside and jumped in front of the police and told them what Jazon had done and the paramedics pushed the police out of the way and tried to examine Jazon but her was wild by then, his mind gone. My father grabbed him in his arms and whispered to him. "Ajay is going to be fine, now rest son I got you".

Jazon had lost all but one percent of all of his bodies blood, by all medical knowledge he should have died, but he refused to die before he finished his task, which that time was to save me" Ajay explained as tears ran down his face.

Silky was crying as well, she cuddled Ajay.

"What happened to the boy how almost killed you" Silky asked?

"The grounds keeper of the school witnessed the entire thing and called the police when they jumped me, when Jazon showed up he thought we were both dead, but Jazon took them apart literally. All three of them never walked again; two are unable to move below the neck although everything still works, their motor skills are permanently shot. The other one Jazon stabbed in the back, his spinal cord was severed. Jazon would have went to jail and the families were going to sue until the school security camera showed the entire show, then it was my family and Jazon's who sued and those boy went to jail for 18 months for attempted murder. Jazon spent five weeks in a coma, his heart stopped three times and I never left his room the whole time. When he opened his eyes for the first time, it was the first day of our new life as brothers. I will never abandon him, not even if it costs me my life. He was willing to die for me with no second thought, can I do less? You want to know how tough he is; Jazon is as mean and tough as he needs to be to win, I

SHANE

have drug him home covered in blood more than once, but nobody ever faced off with Jazon by choice, he is a madman they say. He taught me to fight and feel no pain until later, when it was over. Focus on the task nothing more exists until then" Ajay explained.

"Wow".

"Yes, it carried over and go my into college on a football ride and then off to the pro's and the good life; all because I learned to focus on the prize/ goal whatever, never the struggle" Ajay said.

(Elsewhere in the house).

Terry was moaning in terrible pain, the silver knives were covered in silver nitrate and it was in his blood stream, killing him. Even Pegi was not sure what should be done. Jazon staggered in about to drop and sat on the only chair in the room.

"Jesus, Mary and Joseph, you look about ready to die" Pegi said.

"I need fresh blood pretty bad, Pat is on his way to the drop zone, from there is has to be brought here. So I am waiting, dying right here" Jazon answered.

Enoch was about to cry he felt so helpless over Terry's condition. Pegi looked vexed and worried by the look. Jazon startled them when he spoke.

"Terry quit pussing out and transform now before it is too late and you die. Is the warrior I fought with going to roll up and die or **FIGHT AND BE A MAN**" Jazon yelled!

"What the hell is a matter with you" Pegi yelled back!

(CRACK>>>ROAR).

Even on the brink of death Terry heard the words of his true friend and ally ordering him to fight and live; so on instinct alone he trusted the voice and turned fast and hard. He whole body felt like it was coming apart, his mind was a mist of pain and agony, but his voice was like a razor; it cut through and made him obey. Terry in full werewolf mode looked down at his leader and friend.

"Go hero, go out the back and run the woods until your so tired you can't go on and them let Enoch carry you home" Jazon said as he own eyes were rolling up in his head.

Terry step forward and squeezed Jazon's knee looking him in the eyes, and then grabbed Enoch and bolted out the door. Jazon dropped over out of the chair and did not move, he had reached his non-combat limit.

Two days later Jazon opened his eyes and found Jax under the covers with him sleeping. He ran his hand down her hard back and held her close. Jax opened her bloodshot eyes and looked on the verge of more tears. She was not afforded a chance. Jazon kissed her and kept on kissing her until she melted into his arms and relaxed there. He finally let her go long enough for her to speak.

"The assassin" Jax asked?

"All dead, but a sad story" Jazon told her.

"What, why" Jax asked?

Jazon explained everything, the chase, the battle, the wounds and Gilly. Jax accepted Gilly's post life apology for his poor conduct. Jax was so happy the Jazon was alive that she would have done whatever he asked at that moment. However, all she wanted was to be in his arms.

Later that day around the hotel dining hall Jazon stood up and told them the entire story again and he included his two promises. Gilly was to be buried a king of the sea, so Jazon needed a suitable boat to burn. Tad offered to tend to that. The leprechauns gave a handful of gold a piece to Gilly's treasure. Jazon added a bottle of old Rum he was saving, all sailors liked rum. So it was Saturday night when the entire hotel of magical creatures and some mermaids met at the mouth of the Columbia River and sent Gilly back to the sea a rich man and one with a new friend. When Gill's boat finally burned up and then sank, Jazon and

SHANE

the family left. The look on Jazon's face was as hard as a diamond.

"One promise down" Jazon said on the way back to Vancouver.

(IN FINNEY"S PRIVATE OFFICE).

Brian was not happy at the lack of word from Gilly. Had the famous assassin finally missed and ran away before Brian could claim his money back or Gilly's life. Even mark who always knew everything was a blank newspaper these days.

"Jc come in here" Brian yelled.

"What do you want" Jc asked in a snotty tone/

Brian hated Jc, but the man was an excellent bodyguard and crazy when mad. His lack of servitude pissed Brian off. If Finney did not have Jc over a barrel, he was sure Jc would kill him or try at the least. Jc was a werewolf and a special one at that. He could assume three forms. A man, a werewolf and a full blown timber-wolf; that you could not tell apart from a plain wolf. This made him able to run the street or woods like a stray and nobody really paid any attention.

"I need you to find out what is going on with Gilly. Go to his house kick the damn door in and question him or kill him. I don't care which, I just want to know if the hunters are dead" Brian said?

"Great, where is that suck ass Mark; why not send him" Jc growled/

"He is too weak to beat up Gilly if it comes to it, and you are not" Brian said logically.

"Fine dead it is then" Jc said as he was leaving.

"Get the information first please" Brian said calmly.

(OUTSIDE OF FINNEY"S OFFICE BUILDING)

    The wolf pack and Jazon mined and set gas drums in and around the build that they knew was Brian Finney's headquarters. They watched Jc go in and then come out. He was a werewolf so he knew they were there before they approached him. Jc was about to shift hen a powerful hand was around his throat and his head was pinned to the building.

"Just listen before I have to kill you" Jazon said.

"Fine, I give my word to listen" Jc said.

    Jazon put him down and Jc looked at Enoch, they know each other obviously. Jc noticed all the wolves and knew all their names except Terry.

"Go ahead man, say your peace man" Jc said.

SHANE

"I am going to go beat the shit out of your boss and then I am going to blow up this building, first I want to make sure Mark is in the office with Brian before I do that" Jazon said.

"Oh he is in there but I can't let you do that man, even if I wanted to: Jc said.

"Demi is dead Jc" Enoch said.

Jc turned to Enoch and looked at him. Jc must have known Enoch well enough to know the man never lies.

"Screw them then, let'em cook" Jc said as he dropped a skateboard and was about to leave.

"Hold it, your not alone anymore Jc, your with us now, if you want" Ajay said?

"I am down with that" Jc said.

First things first before we torch this pit, I have to go visit the owner and his lackey, Jazon thought. He took Ajay be the elbow and walked toward the front door, it was locked. Enoch walked forward and ripped it off the hinges. Now Enoch knew Jazon was as strong as or even stronger than him, he just did not want the Vampire to waste his strength after coming to close to dying so recently. Terry still had not recovered completely, but Jazon was right about Terry; when Terry ran the adrenaline and healing in his werewolf's blood burned the silver out of him and saved his life. Ajay drank the elixir of life and healed up pretty well despite the damage. Jazon has on the other hand

SHANE

literally bleed to death and it too a few days to ascertain if they could even save him. They put literally five gallons of blood into Jazon before he woke up and then tears of blood ran from his eyes.

"Well done Enoch" Jc said.

"You boys need to wolf out before we go up stairs and if you find any wolves in here or any non-vampires, get them out even if you have to beat their ass to do it. This party is for Brian and Mark alone" Jazon said in a gruff voice.

Ajay went first shotgun at the ready, Jazon wanted to go next but Enoch and Terry closed in behind Ajay like sentinels. Biz walked with Jazon, they had become chess mates over the week after the stadium. Behind then Jc and the rest of the wolves stalked in. Jazon could feel the malice in Jc's mind and his body was vibrating with hate.

"Watch it, we are not alone" Ajay said as he dropped the safety on his gun.

Terry put his hand on Ajay's should looked at him from 3 feet above him and pointed to the floor. Terry walked passed Ajay and went in the room on the right where Ajay felt there was an ambush coming.

(ROAR).

Three werewolves hit the wall in the hallway, nearly senseless. Enoch grabbed them snarled something in wolf to them and tossed them toward the exit, they staggered out of the building; taking human form at the door. Terry came out of the room dragging a dead vampire, the head was in Terry's left clawed hand and the heart was on the floor. Terry flung the body out the window.

"Damn, Terry" Ajay said!

Terry had grown as a person and a warrior since his near death experience. It humbled him; all the lessons Enoch tried to teach him came home and grew inside of Terry. He was once a good fighter, now he was a force of nature, and completely loyal to Jazon, he appointed himself bodyguard and protector of Jazon; God help anyone who tried to interfere with that. Terry remembered when he was helpless Jazon protected him at great cost to himself and when he was dying of Silver poison; it was Jazon who knew what he had to do just to live. Jazon proved himself to be trustworthy and more than that a hero, a Vampire Hero. Who would have believed that since vampires are by nature evil.

Terry lead the way up the stairs and ripped every camera off the wall as they went, to keep the vampires up stairs blind. Brian Finney was no fool but even he was not match for this bunch. On the fourteenth floor, there were no wolves; just vampires and they were armed and dangerous. One jumped on Enoch and sank his teeth into the big Werewolf's neck. Blood sprayed all over the floor and the vampire was to lost in blood lust to see Jc run up the wall and drop on the vampire like a Mack truck. Jc crushed the life out of the hapless vampire and then ripped his heart out and head off in slow motion. Jc really hated vampires. Enoch was fine after a few minutes a little dizzy from the vampire venom; which contrary to popular belief does nothing to werewolves but make them dizzy. The werewolf blood blocks and defeats the vampire venom. It works the other way as well, a vampire bitten by a Werewolf will not turn into a wolf; their blood opposes one another.

 "Look out" Ajay screamed as three vampire dropped through the ceiling and on to Jazon.

   Jazon did not pull his blades; he snapped his razor claws out and rent the three vampires apart in less than a minute, every time his hand went across their bodies something else was torn off. Jazon was the only Vampire any of the wolves ever seen to have...well, werewolf claws. Jazon was just as good at using them as any wolf was, likely much better since he was a kungfu guy. Blood dripped from Jazon's face as he started up the stairs to the fifteenth and last floor.

   Brian Finney was not a fool, he did not his building was under siege and was ready for the intruders when they got there. He did not plan on Jazon and his hunter shadow and the seven werewolves that were under his control. Finney thought more like human crime lords or another Vampire alpha, but this was not the case. Mark was stationed behind the door with a P-90 assault rifle, fully auto.

Since this was night time Finney's office building was pretty much clear except a few foolish vampires and enslaved werewolves. Ajay was about to pass Jazon at the huge double office doors when both a vampire hand and a huge Werewolf clawed hand were on his chest stopping him dead in his tracks. The wolf sniffed the air, so did Jazon.

"The door is booby trapped and we are expected. I think it would be rude not to knock don't you" Jazon pointed to the doors?

(THE PACK AND JAZON LAUGHED)

"Back up little big brother" Jazon said.

Terry and Jazon stood side by side and on Jazon's three count; they kicked both doors complete off the hinges, which was hard because they were solid metal with re-enforced bindings. The mangled doors landed right next to Brian's desk. There was a minor explosion and plenty of dust.

"OH SHIT" Mark said from the side!

Jazon looked at Ajay and the wolves and gave a stern command, brooking no argument.

"Stay out of the room, if Mark shoot me kill him Ajay, if Brian kills me make damn sure his never sees another day, other than that stay out" Jazon said in a low tone.

Brian could see only the glowing eyes of the wolves and two piercing white ones in the dark dusty aftermath of the explosion. He agreed with mark when he could see what and who was coming into his room. Brian reached for his sword and found the new arrival's hand on top of his.

"I don't think so. Either remove your hand or I will...from your body" Jazon said.

"You have a set on you to come in here and threaten me" Brian said.

Jazon's hand changed and became clawed which his sank into Brian's hand crushing and ripping it up at the same time. Brian could not believe the insane power this vampire had.

"Very well, I will yield for the moment" Brian said reluctantly.

When Jazon let his hand up, Brian took his hand away. Jazon tossed Finney's sword across the room away from Brian and Mark. Mark was about to move when Ajay cleared his throat.

"Drop the gun punk or I will fill you full of silver shot and hard wood pellets" Ajay said with a mean smile.

Mark is no fool, shotgun versus machine gun, the shotgun will win a close range and they were at close range. Mark tossed his gun away.

"Drop all your weapons, blades, everything or I will just shoot you" Ajay told him.

Mark made a sour face, but he complied. As it turned out Mark had a great deal of weapons on his person. Mark back up against the wall and stood there looking disgruntle.

"Why have you invaded my office, and come to your prince unbidden" Brain said in a haughty tone!

The werewolves laugh in a growling rolling tone. Ajay chuckled and Jazon was not amused.

"That was partly the correct question, and partly the wrong stance. You are no more than a mangy dog to be put down trash can. You are no prince to us. I came here because you are an idiot. You sent an assassin after me without knowing enough about me to understand the barrel of whup-ass it would open. I am here to collect on the debts owed Finney" Jazon said.

Finney made a sour face as if he was confused and cross about it.

"What makes you think I owe you anything, what possible debt could I owe you" Brian asked/

Finney did not like being on the receiving end of things, he liked to dictate.

"You don't owe me jack shit you pompous dickhead, I am here to collect on the debt owed to...GILLY" Jazon said.

In a movement so fast only Brian Finney saw it coming; Jazon pulled Gilly's Bowie knife and hurled it across the room and into the chest of Mark O'Day. It went right into the hardwood wall behind mark and pinned him there like a bug pinned to a board on display. Mark gargles as blood ran out his mouth.

"Gilly made me promise to give you his knife Mark and I promised him I would give it to you, and so I have, item one complete. Now on to you Brian Finney, you insect. You have ruled the coast for too long by the strength of your sword arm, which I think is over rated, by the arm you right or left handed" Jazon asked?

"I am right handed, my left is useless with a blade" Brian said.

If not for the fact that Mark snickered Jazon may not have known that Brian was lying. In a flash, Jazon was over the desk and hand Brian down, Jazon sank his teeth into Brian's neck and ripped his throat open and tasted his blood. He grabbed Brain's left arm and ripped it off his body, and then snapped the bones his right arm and left leg. He tossed Brian in the middle of the room and then knelt down beside him.

SHANE

"I am not going to kill you Brian Finney or even that little prick Mark. I am going to ruin your world, bring down your empire and rule this region as protector from here on out. All the werewolves are mine and will not serve you anymore. If you live leave here with your life and never return or I will kill you" Jazon said.

Jazon walked over and picked up Brian's left arm and turned to the wolves and Ajay who all had shocked faces.

"What" Jazon asked?

"Look into that mirror man" Ajay said.

Jazon walked to the mirror on the wall and saw his reflection, it was not one he recognized. His ears were pointed, he had four fangs, two upper and two shorter ones on the bottom. His eyes and ear were pointed and his eyes red crimson with white pupils. The muscles in his neck were engorged and as his looked down so were the rest of the muscles in his body. No wonder he was able to rip Brian's arm off so easily. He was not sure why he was so changed, but it likely tipped the scale of power in his favor. No matter, Finney was going to burn and so was Mark.

"We are out of here" Ajay said as Jazon walked passed him and down the stairs.

When Jazon and his crew were gone, Finney crawled over to his desk and climbed up it and into his chair. He dialed his phone and told the person in the phone what had happened and asked for help, which was distasteful to him.

(OUTSIDE FINNEY"S OFFICE BUILDING)

Ajay watched as Jazon became himself again and Terry opened a fire hydrant so Jazon could clean the blood off of himself and anyone else whom needed to do just that.

"Burn it down Ajay" Jazon yelled from across the street.

Ajay had three special shells that Pegi made for him, they were white phosphorus and they really lit a fire if you fire them. They also cleaned Ajay's shotgun barrel out, he could only fire one at a time, two in a row would mess up his weapon.

"My pleasure little brother" Ajay hollered back!

(KA-BOOM)

The entire bottom floor exploded into flames. The Wolves had mined the building as they climbed in earlier, therefore once the flames tickled the gas bombs on the second floor they went off as well and so on.

SHANE

"What they hell is that" Screamed Brian Finney!

Vampires are as vulnerable to fire as any other creature and it hurts them just as much as it would you if you were on fire. So when flames began to grow up the stairs and covered the windows from outside Brian was terrified. His body was broken and his only friend pinned to the wall dying. Brian was trying to decided whether or not to go and attempt to save Mark when there was a major explosion that shattered the windows for ten blocks, and Brian's building crumble to the ground with the two vampire still inside.

SHANE

VAMPIRE HERO SAGA

SHANE

CHAPTER 12: ROAD TRIP

In the days that followed the assault on Brian's office tower, the magical community were at peace for the first time in nearly seventy years. The local crime bosses, with a lack of supervision decided to make war on each other. Jazon met with the heads of the largest vampire clans from Seattle to Eugene and advised them if they felt compelled to take down the criminal organization, by drinking them dry, he and his bigger family would look the other way for six months. However, if they attacked an innocent, he would set the wolves on them or visit himself with his two shadows.

"We will take this one time six month open window to deal with the human scum who help dilute our blood supply with drugs and poisons. We will kill them off and take their places" One older vampire said.

"Do you speak for the group Alister" Jazon asked?

Around the room the many leaders looked at Alister and gave him the thumbs up. He turned back to Jazon and Ajay, and he seemed to think about what he wanted to say.

"They are in agreement with me in this matter, but I can't speak for them about other items not currently on the table" Alister said.

SHANE

Ajay smiled and so did Jazon and Terry. They liked this man, vampire aside. Alister was wise and long lived and respected by all who knew him. It would appear he did not get crossed either, apparently he was very strict when it came to pay back, if you crossed him, then you died for it. Pretty simple, NO?

"What, have I said something off colored or inappropriate" Alister asked?

"Not at all Alister; we find your use of caution and thoughtful response to be very admirable" Ajay said.

"Very good, might I make a suggestion Jazon" Alister asked?

"Yes of-course Alister, what would you like to suggest" Jazon asked?

Alister explained how Brian had ruled the coast, by proxy and only once in awhile did he make a face to face appearance. Alister thought it would be prudent to have a face to face with the three most powerful vampires in California. If they were well cautioned to behave, then the rest of the lower level vampire lords would fall into line, because if they crossed you; the greater lords would crush them to avoid you coming to their domains. Therefore, the peace is not kept by Jazon and his crew; but by the vampires who rule the region. This seemed to Ajay and Tad to be an excellent suggestion and sage advice.

"Great advice Alister; would you like to do the introductions" Jazon asked?

"Yes, I am willing to do that" Alister answered.

(LATER BACK AT HOTEL MAGIC)

Preparations for a road trip were being made all night. Pegi was cooking and making some serious medical ointments for the boys before they left, just incase they ran par for course and ended up fighting for their lives as usual.

Silky was pissed that Ajay was going to leave her behind, but she could see the wisdom of it; even though her heart hurt at being separated from her big chocolate daddy. Ajay told her they would take a holiday when he got back. Not fighting just fun in the sun or snow, or where ever Silky wanted to go. Silky was happy and excited, she began making plans just after that.

Jax who watched Jazon being put back together and saw the damage and witnessed her man dying from blood loss, was doing everything she could to keep Jazon from leaving her behind. Jazon was heart sick about leaving his true love behind but, this trip was close to a declaration of war, and as such Jax could not be anywhere near when the pooh hit the fan.

SHANE

"Jax I need you to run the club, and help Pegi run the hotel. Father Sully is going to need you to manage the funds and the shipment because you're human" Jazon explained.

Jax did not want to hear those words but she knew it was right, she was needed here to help the greater good. She gave in but told Jazon he could not leave until he wore her out sexually. Jazon chuckled and told her it would be his pleasure.

(AT BREAKFAST THEN NEXT MORNING)

The dining hall was full of damn near everyone in the greater magical – mythical community. They all came to hear or see Jazon, the vampire who brought tradition and then broke Brian Finney's tyranny. Jazon had a fine ham and egg breakfast and a beaker of bovine blood slightly salted with garlic. When he had finished he stood up and spoke.

"Attention please; I am Jazon Wild and I am loosely the leader of the magical creature community and surrounding areas. I want to thank you for coming today. I have to leave town and meet some less than happy vampires about my expectations. While I am gone I am leaving a few key persons to look after whatever pops up. Pegi the Elf-witch will be in charge of the hotel, with Enoch. Silky and Jax will coordinate

SHANE

all the budget and shipments to the hotel with father Sully, Biz will be looking after their security. All complaints or requests will be made though Tad who is very wise, he will be partnered with Wolf, who all of you respect, please keep all issues friendly. Lastly, Jc will take out the wolf pack and be the sheriff while I am gone. If there is a vampire attack or anything else call for Jc and he will come to your aid" Jazon explained.

"Hey how long are you going to be gone anyway" Block asked?

"Not so long I will miss the mushroom soup you promised to make us" Jazon teased the troll.

The entire dining hall laughed. Block made damn good soup and was shy about it because he did not think so. It made the powerful immortal blush after a fashion, and that is why everyone always laughed. Block was adored by all the magical creatures.

"One additional thing, we are a huge family. Yes, we are, and as such we must come together and work together for a better world for us all to live in. If you're a ogre or troll, faerie or a mermaid, you all have to try to help each other in everyway, so that one day we can all walk around in the open and enjoy being free" Jazon said.

(4PM FLIGHT TO LA)

SHANE

Alister paid for the first class tickets to California. Strangely for the airline the entire plane was bought out, every seat paid for but only first class had any people in it.

A family who had a sick son in college in LA came and asked Alister if he would allow them to seat in economy if they could go along, they said we will pay triple. Alister was going to say no, but Ajay interrupted him.

"You will pay nothing; we will be glad to help you reach you ill child and you can sit in first class if you like" Ajay said.

Alister looked like he was going to protest but Terry was already ushering the family onto the plane. Jazon and Ajay seemed to be of one mind on everything. Suddenly, Alister understood just how dangerous Ajay really was. The human was said to have faced down Vampires alone and prevailed against a dozen or so. What was this human made of to make him so foolhardy, or just to brave for good judgment. Alister thought he understood the bonds that held Jazon's family together; they were love and respect not fear and punishment.

"You look ill Alister, if it was the cost of the tickets, I will cover their cost. I seized Brian Finney's assets, so I am quite wealthy at present and I am going to expect a certain amount of tribute for operating in my regions, but not much. Wait, your thinking because I am kind that I wont be strong enough to hold the balance of power, that would be a mistake Alister, I killed Finney with my bare hands, remember that" Jazon said.

Alister boarded the plane behind Jazon and the rest of the crew. The flight was short but active. The two clans mingled and found they got along well and even enjoyed the company of one another. The family that shared the ride were confused at the conversations going back and forth about werewolves versus vampires abilities, such as who healed faster and so on. Ajay looked after the family and told them that the plane was full of fantasy geeks on their way to a meeting of more fantasy fans. The family bought it because the alternative would have meant something to horrible to believe. They were on a plane filled to the brim with vampires and werewolves...

(BACK AT HOTEL MAGICAL)

There was a knock on the door and it was the Vancouver Police. Jax was at the church with Father Sully taking care of buying food and fabric for the hotel personal. A dwarf saw the police and ran for it. He rammed into one of Enoch's legs and fell on his little butt.

SHANE

"Hey wolfface, there are cops at the front door" The dwarf yelled.

Enoch started toward the front door and Pegi yelled from the kitchen.

"HALT Enoch, I will answer the door" Pegi said.

"Okay but I am with you incase they need to be killed" Enoch said all possessively.

Pegi smiled at him, but as she walked she grabbed a old lady dress out of the closet and she stopped and striped butt naked and then put the dress on. The dwarf was wowed by Pegi's hot young body; Enoch was just confused by Pegi's actions. That is until she walked toward the door and became an old woman of seventy years or so. Pegi opened the door and addressed the police.

"Yes can I help you boys" Older Pegi asked?

"Yes, we are looking for a man named Ajay Rey the football player, he was reported coming here last night" The officer stated.

"Yes, he was here his girlfriend Silky lives here. I am sorry to say he is not currently here, he left for California at 4PM with his best friend Jazon on personal business" Pegi explained.

The police looked at each other and they were trying to decide how to proceed. They decided wrong.

"Well then we will just come in and look around for ourselves granny to make sure you didn't just tell us a fib" The cop said snotty.

"No you will not. If you don't have a search warrant, then you can piss off. If you try to force your way in then he and his brothers will stop you" Pegi said kicking the door all the way open to show a giant Enoch and six other werewolves standing behind her, all close to 7 foot tall.

The police stepped back and one reach for his gun. Biz was standing behind them and put his hand over the pistol and shook his head no. Enoch and Jc were standing looking down at the police with a parental posture.

"Boys, you are trespassing. If you're looking for our boy Ajay why don't you call his cell phone and ask him where he is" Jc told them.

"Would you be willing to get us his cell number" The cop asked?

Silky had been listening and she speed dialed Ajay and walked out and handed her phone to the police officer, who looked at the beautiful girl and nearly drooled.

"Wow no wonder he comes here. Mr. Rey this is the Vancouver Police, where are you sir, we have reports that you were kidnapped" The police stated.

("I am on a United air flight with my boy Jazon to LA, I will be home in a few days. Who the hell called you again" Ajay asked over the phone?)

"It was your coach, he thinks your being held against your will and so he called the police for your protection" The cop explained.

("What an idiot, you tell that baboon I will be there for the playoff and stop busting my hump, not give my baby back her phone" Ajay said in disgust.)

The police officer gave the phone back; Silky took it and spoke softly as she walked away to her man. Enoch and Jc stood there looking at the police now with open contempt.

"Shame on you for threatening to force your way into the old ladies hotel. Make sure if you ever come back to be polite to the staff of this hotel, or you may very well loose your badge; now if you have no more business here we will bid you a good day" Jc said as he blew a bubble with his gum.

"Yes of-course; we are sorry to bother you, have a nice day" The police officer said as they left in a hurry.

Enoch walked in to the house and Pegi was in the middle of changing clothes and ages as Jc and Enoch watched. Jc was wowed by Pegi's suddenly super hot young body, because he had never actually met her. Enoch waited for Pegi to put on her shorts and baby doll tee before he spoke to her. Pegi saw that Enoch wanted to ask her something, so she spirited him away to the kitchen.

"How did you do that" Enoch asked?

"Do what"?

"You are young and you became old and then young again" Enoch explained his question?

"Oh. Enoch I am two hundred and five years old actually, I just reverted for a moment to answer the door, and now I generated back to my younger self" Pegi explained.

Enoch still looked confused; so Pegi kissed him on the cheek and made a funny comment.

"Enoch let me put it this way; 'NO ONE WANTS TO GO DOWN ON A TUMBLE WEED'; so I prefer to wear my younger form, but the older body and look is also very pleasant and useful. Does that explain it well enough" Pegi giggled?

"Tumble weed, Jesus Mary and Joseph" Enoch laughed.

(LAX AIRPORT)

Alister was shocked and surprised how gentle these people were, yet the same group utterly destroyed the tyrant Brian Finney in a single stroke. Alister would make very careful arrangements to never fall into Jazon's cross-hairs. Ajay was another matter; Alister had never seen a pure human with this level of courage and valor. Moreover, the werewolves follow this man and his shadow not as slaves but as fiercely loyal friends. Friends, who would have thought this was possible?

Jazon and Terry were chatting off to the side when Ajay walked up.

"I think there is more to the story than Ajay's coach worrying about him" Terry said.

"Right, I agree let's finish out tasks here and go home and watch out for our own family, because I think there is something up as well" Jazon said.

Ajay listened in silence, he was already primed to blow after his call with Silky. Someone send the fuzz to scope out our hotel for weakness, he was sure of it. However, he came down here to help keep the peace; therefore Ajay was not about to whine to Jazon about going home even though that is all he wanted right at the moment. Ajay snuck in a call to Block and Wolf, he told them that he thought there was some poop coming and to be sure to not let anyone near Jax or Silky. Wolf told Ajay he did have a bad feeling and would keep his eye on the ball at all times.

Alister had a limo waiting to take them to the private dinner being held for Jazon and company. They arrived at a hotel as big as twenty city blocks and plush would be an insult to the splendor of it all. Terry was awe struck, but Jazon was not. He looked like he was ready for War. Alister suddenly began to have anxiety grow in his stomach; he quashed it and forged ahead. The new arrivals were lead to a remote dining area for VIP's only.

"Wait" Terry said at the doors.

Terry took a deep breath and opened the doors and snarled as a full werewolf, all the vampires jumped in fright they had not been notified that Jazon was bringing Wolves with him, and this one caught them by surprise and he was big. Jazon walked in and put his hand on Terry's shoulder as the guards jumped back in terror.

"My friend does not trust people who stand behind doors. We have recently had quite a lot of that and would like to put a stop to that practice" Jazon said.

Alister walked in and the three vampire lords around the table began to yell at him all at once, Alister did not react at all. Terry had enough of this bologna and stopped it cold.

(SNARL)!!!!

SHANE

The room reverberated with the sheer volume of Terry's roar, he sound more lion an angry tiger or lion than a wolf, but the message was clear enough; shut up or else. Terry reverted to human form and stood looking at the leaders with open hostility.

"I can change in less than a second gentlemen so don't get cute or I will get ugly, I promise" Terry said with a malicious smile.

"Tell you slave to behave or get out fledgling" a fat vampire named Orson said.

Terry was about to change and Jazon put a restraining hand on his arm and held him there. Ajay stepped forward and gave the lords a second big shock.

"We are not amused fat ass, Terry is Jazon's body guard by choice not orders, if he wants to leave or come and go, that is his solo choice. Just this once; are we going to ask him to make peace, after this you're on your own" Ajay explained in a flat tone.

The vampires looked at each other and sniffed the air.

"Is this black kid to be an offer to the counsel of peace" Lars asked hopefully?

If you feel frosty baby come and try to bite me, but I only think it would be fair to warn you I bite back" Ajay said.

"Would you two retards please keep your mouths shut while I speak with the guests" Robert said to the other vampire lords!

Alister looked ill as Robert got up and sniffed Ajay. Robert reached out a hand slowly and touched Ajay along his ribs and smiled as he took his hand away. Robert looked at Jazon and approach him as well with his hand extended. Jazon shook his hand.

"Welcome Jazon to my hotel, would you please dine with me, while we talk about our new arrangement for trade items, and cash flow" Robert said calmly with a smile.

The host pointed to some seats. Ajay and Jazon sat with Alister who left his guards outside for good measure. Terry stood behind Jazon's chair and looked ready to pounce at a moments notice. Jazon on the other hand looked at peace.

"Nice crib man" Ajay said to Robert.

"Thank you; it is one of five hotels here in the west. I am not allowed business out of my region without war" Robert told him.

Robert clapped his hands and the curtains opened and naked girls brought in the food and beakers of blood and wine.

Ajay reached out to take a steak off the platter and Orson grabbed his hand; like lightning Ajay had his shotgun pistol in the fat vampire's mouth.

SHANE

"Remove your hand from my arm or I will remove your head" Ajay growled!

"I am a vampire, bullets won't kill me" Orson said.

(LAUGHTER)

"You had better take a good sniff before he pulls the trigger jumbo, or it has been nice knowing you" Robert said as he laughed.

Lars sniffed the air and his eyes grew huge, Orson smelled the shells and started to tremble. If Ajay had pulled the trigger, he would have been permanently dead, not just injured. Who was this man and why is he here?

"Let us eat and be friends" Alister said/

"Here, here, I say we eat and be merry, no more fighting at the table. Orson behave yourself in my house; last warning" Robert said.

Robert winked at Jazon; who smiled and shook his head as he took a steak as well and a glass of blood. Human blood. Jazon spit it out.

"No offense Robert but I have swore not to drink the blood of man, I drink only animal blood, but I would not mind having Rootbeer instead with my steak" Jazon said.

SHANE

"Hey us too" Said Terry.

With a smile as he reached passed Ajay to a plate on the table and deposited a piece of bread and three chicken legs, a sausage link, and a steak. Terry lifted a knife and fork as well and began to eat slowly.

"You taught him table manners" Lars asked in earnest?

"What, my mother taught me table manners bloodsucker. Just because I am a powerful werewolf does not mean I can get by acting like an animal. There is no telling when manners might save your life or stop a battle" Terry explained.

Alister smiled in agreement, so did Robert. Alister thought to himself, what a strange crew this new vampire overlord has, so powerful and yet very human and innocent in a way as well.

"While we eat; let us get down to it. I will pay you the 40% I paid Finney; to not have you pull a Finney on me. I do not want to be burnt alive and ripped apart Jazon" Robert said.

"I will take 20% and free lodgings at any and all of your hotels when I am or any of my crew are staying with you. Agreed" Jazon offered/

"You want less not more, that is bad business son. But yes I accept your terms" Robert answered.

Jazon turned on the other two vampire lords but addressed Alister.

"How much were they paying Brian" Jazon asked as he took another bite of steak?

"35% from both of their clans" Alister answered.

"It is now 40% until you learn to mind you manners and respect my crew. Or I can slaughter all of you and have my people take over, you decide" Jazon said casually?

"This is an outrage" Orson snarled!

"I will pay" Lars answered.

Jazon turned to Robert.

"You are in charge down here, if there is a problem handle it and I will leave the admin shit to you. If you can't handle I will come down here and handle in severally" Jazon said. "For looking after things Robert I am giving you the 20% discount on your payments. Make me proud".

"WHY THE HELL SHOULD WE PAY THIS CHILD" Orson screamed!

Jazon sighed and went to speed. He had Orson dangling by his fat neck at the end of Jazon's small left arm. Just when you might think the show was over, Jazon throttle the vampire like a rag doll, Jazon looked at Orson and then he throttled him again for good measure.

"If you ever cross me or move against me again, I will pull your arms out of the sockets and beat you to death with them. I killed Brian Finney because he threatened my family, do you think you can succeed where he failed Orson" Jazon said with pure white eyes with little red pupils?

"N nnnnnno sir" Orson cried.

Jazon put him down and smiled; he walked back around the table and opened another Rootbeer and drank some. Robert was not laughing this time, he was I shock.

"Very well done sir" Alister whispered.

Orson got up and so did Lars, they walked by Jazon and stopped; toss him a curt bow; then split form the hotel all together. When they were confirmed gone from the area Robert opened up like a spring flower.

"GOD, I hate those guys! All they do is complain, if you would give me the go ahead I would kill both of them. But wait, how did you throttle Orson like that one handed, he is 450lbs at the least and he is as strong as three vampires by himself; which is why he is the leader of his clan. Lars is no coward but he was scared after you tossed Orson around with no effort" Robert asked?

(LAUGHTER FROM TERRY, AJAY AND JAZON)

Ajay was the first to gather his wits.

"Jazon is very special, he is stronger and faster than most vampires and he has some extra special abilities, but I won't say what those are" Ajay said.

Robert made a serious face and then busted out laughing.

"It would be a mistake to under estimate any of you, Alister was correct to not oppose you. You seem to be a fair man and have a good crew backing you up. I am with you not against you Jazon, but Lars and Orson will not be, there will be blood; mark my word" Robert said.

An hour later Alister and the boys were on a plane heading back to Portland Oregon or PDX airport and then on to the hotel and their girls. Alister told Jazon he wanted to run Jazon's local business interests and he would cover the funds and make it all look and feel legitimate, so that Jazon could just live a good life and not have to worry about anything but laying down the law.

CHAPTER 13: LAST STRAW.

Pegi had the Hotel running well and Father Sully was a great help to the magical community; the good Father made sure the food and medical supplies were always delivered himself. He gave the best daily worship for God's servant that most of the folks had ever had the chance to hear. It gave them hope and a feeling of well being.

It was unknown why it happened or who sent them but the hotel was attacked at just the right time.

The morning of the day after Jazon left for California, Father Sully called Pegi and told her that she was needed and so were the werewolves to load and bring in the heavy items they ordered at the warehouse, such as the new water heater and boiler. So Pegi and Enoch grabbed the big truck and went down to help Sully get it all together and bring it back to the hotel. Wolf and Biz went with Silky and Jax to the club as security during the pay check hand out ritual. After Jax was assaulted by Gilly; Wolf and Biz made damn sure she was never left alone, especially now that Brian was killed;

revenge was bound to spring up.

(AT HOTEL MAGICAL)

A figure shrouded in black hung in the shadows, it watched and listened as all the powerful monsters left the hotel except two. Jc walked out the front door to get the paper and was hit seven times with tranquilizer darts powerful enough to kill an elephant, but Jc was a werewolf not an elephant so he did not die, he just passed. To intruders ran into the hotel and set it on fire and blocked the exits. Little did they know that during the day most of the residents were not in the hotel, they worked or roamed as their nature called for. Therefore, they did not have practically anyone to injure or burn.

"Who dares to burn my home" Yelled Block!

The big troll came barreling through the wall since the door was blocked and he saw the raging fire and did something rarely ever seen. Block blew spores out of his head, and body. The spores instantly put out the fire. Block was hit with a handful of darts, he turned on his attacker, but the shooter melted into the smoke and was gone. Block save the hotel but it was damaged.

(AT CLUB PARADICE, 45 MINUTES LATER)

"Okay here are your checks girls and Mr. Wild has granted you all a PHAT bonus this month don't spend it all in one play" Jax said.

The girls all laughed and some flirted with Wolf or Biz but they all finally left and went home or to the bank or where ever; leaving Wolf and the others alone.

"Well thank God Jazon will be back today, I don't like running things" Jax said.

"Oh come on Jazon says you run everything all the time anyway, you just miss him in your arms and in your bed" Silky said with a giggle.

(KA-BOOM)

A bullet hit Biz in the back of his head and he was forward flipped on to the ground, blood rushed from his head all over the ground.

(SNARL)

Wolf was hit by both bullets and tranquilizer darts at the same time, he was unable to transform but he did not go down, he jumped in front of the girls protectively even though blood was gushing out of his chest and abdomen. Even Silky did not know Wolf was a were wolf because he was not like the other Wolves; Wolf was a normal sized man, not a giant, but right now both girls could feel a new strength in this man.

"Cowards, come out and fight in the open" Wolf screamed!

A bullet hit Wolf in the forehead flinging him into Jax. They fell together on to the ground. Wolf's body pinned Jax to the ground. A dark clad figure came out of the shadows and made a beeline right for the unguarded Silky. The figure grabbed her arm and pulled out a syringe and injected Silky with something. The Wood nymph gasped and would have collapsed but the figure held her up.

"Don't worry little one you won't die right away. But I am not after you; you see I wish to kill a man, no make that two men and I needed to get to you or her" The figure said pointing at Jax who was struggling on the ground. "They will be insane with anger and will follow me anywhere I go to get the antidote and kill me, but they won't be able to do either of those things; because I will be waiting and I will kill them".

(CLICK CLICK BOOM)

Jax shot the figure in the chest with her special made 9MM, and then she shot him or her again and again. She riddled the figure as they turned to flee gargling blood.

SHANE

"Please God help me" Jax cried.

Silky who was in the greatest agony Jax has ever saw crawled over and helped Jax get Wolf's dead body off of her. Jax was on her knees when Silky collapsed into her. Jax held her friend as Silky's eyes began to drift shut; Jax shook her violently to keep her awake.

"I'm sorry Jax that I am not strong like you, I can't keep fighting; I am dying and my only comfort is that my best friend was here at the end with me so I don't have to die alone" Silky said.

The wood nymph closed her eyes and her heart stopped. Jax threw her head back and screamed so loud the windows in the building shattered, and then she cried her heart out. Around Jax lay her friends all dead, Jax was alone.

(AT THE HOTEL)

Enoch could smell the flames and smoke before the truck even got close to the hotel, he startled Pegi and Mick when he ripped the door to the truck open and dove out. He was a full werewolf when he touched the ground and he accelerated to a speed no truck to could match and was gone. Pegi stomped on the gas and Mick yelled to the Wolves in the back of the truck holding the equipment and supplies to hold on. The scene Pegi beheld when the truck came around the bend to the hotel made her heart lurch.

"Everyone out search for injured and fire make sure it is contained" Mick ordered.

Father Sully had searched as a chaplain in the Army during the Viet Nam war, so he knew what had to happen and made sure it did. There were very few injured and Block killed the fire before any real damage could be done. Block already had water sprites and a bog monster which love ash and soot cleaning the walls and ceiling to rid the hotel of the smoke smell.

"Nothing, and nobody to punish" Enoch roared in anger!

Pegi's face suddenly went ash grey and then pale.

"OMG, where is Jax and Silky" Pegi gasped?

Something stirred behind them and then a pissed off voice spoke with gravel in his throat.

"They went to the Paradice club to hand out the pay checks to the girls. They are in danger no doubt about it. Enoch you're with me" Jc said as he transformed.

The two Werewolves went to speed and they were straining to pick up even more speed, since their friends and charges were in danger. What they found when they got there made Enoch cry and Jc howl in anguish. They controlled their own pain and Enoch carried Biz and Wolf's lifeless bodies back to the hotel.

SHANE

Jc lifted Jax up and carried her, because Silky's tiny limp body was cradled in her arms already and she was not about to let her friend go. The werewolves walked slowly in the alleys and back roads back to the hotel with anger and pain crushing the life out of them. But there was one more common drive among the friends REVENGE!

(TWO HOURS LATER AT THE HOTEL)

Alister's limo drove up to the hotel and Jazon got out, Terry leaped straight through the sunroof and landed on the ground outside and then he ran in the small wooded area. Ajay looked at he friends confused; until Jazon turned and looked at him with silver white eyes and red pupils. Ajay ripped out of the limo shotgun in hand ready to fight.

Pegi walked out of the hotel with her eyes red from crying and she took Jazon and Ajay's hands and lead them into the building and up the stairs. Jazon's heart was hardly even beating, but each beat was hard and painful in his chest. Ajay looked about to explode from anxiety, he must have thought it was Jax who was injured by Jazon's face, he was so terribly wrong.

"I am sorry, I was to slow to stop this" Block said from the floor where the big troll sat lifelessly.

Pegi opened the door and pulled the boys in behind her. There were three beds, two of them had bodies covered by sheets, the third contained Jax who was wrapped around Silky.

"What happened" Ajay whispered unable to find any volume while holding his breath?

Pegi just looked at him and tried to speak but instead she fell apart and sagged to the floor in misery. Pegi had tried to be strong and lead the family, but her tender heart was broken and she could not go on. Enoch who had been in the corner silent as death move forward and swept Pegi up into his massive arms; Enoch too had red swollen eyes from weeping.

A figure stumbled forward.

"We were ambushed J, they came for us when we were apart and vulnerable, they studies us. They waited until you and my bro were out of town and then they pounced on us" Jc said in anger.

The wild Wolf looked sick and not from grief. Jc noticed Jazon's analyzing stare and spoke.

"I'll live, I have been poisoned; but they under estimated my will to live. I will be paying that bill back, my word on it" Jc said!

"Rest my friend, your chance will come, you have my word on it" Jazon said.

SHANE

Ajay walked over and looked at the girls. He thought they were dead and he could barely keep his head from swimming at the thought of life Without Silky.

"Jazon" Jax scream and jumped off the bed and into his arms from across the room.

Jazon squeezed her so hard that Jax's ribs were buckling but she did not say so, she wanted to feel in vise grip arms around her little body. Jax cried silently with her head buried in Jazon's neck.

"Wake up sleepy head" Ajay said to Silky as he bent and kissed her cold lips.

Silky did not move or even seem to breathe. Ajay was on the verge of hysterical, when a tiny hand pulled on his jeans to get his attention.

"She is not dead Ajay, just in a coma for now. I have tried everything I know to counter the poison, Pegi can't help her either unless she knows what the problem stems from, or we might actually kill Silky trying to save her. Her only chance is to find the culprit and rip the cure out of them before you tear out his black heart" Tad said in a hiss!

"My baby is dying and we need to find the bastard responsible to get the cure; before we can do that, we have to find them period" Ajay howled in despair.

There was such a din coming up the stairs that everyone jumped in to a fighting posture just as Terry vaulted to the top of the stairs as a werewolf. He was so angry and excited he could hardly revert back to a man. He finally made it though and he was gritting his teeth so hard blood was seeping from his mouth.

"Hold the news until we bury our dead" Jazon said.

The far bed began to shake and the sheet blew up and disintegrated. Where there was once a dead boy with a bullet in his head now stood Bizerc the fire demon, with wings were folded back and tucked to his spine. The bullet in his head was forced out of his head by flames and the hole closed. Bizerc's red in red eyes were flashing in barely contained ire.

"Jesus save us and keep us from the devils grip" Father Mick Sully began to pray.

"My GOD, Biz is possessed by a demon" Jax said climbing behind Jazon's back.

"Oh please, like I would consort with that guy. I am; for the record a redeemed soul. I was matched with a dying boy who had a higher destiny than a miserable death, so the All Mighty asked me to merge with the child and let my immortality save the kid, and I have to stay joined for eternity to Biz to preserve his life. Therefore the boy cannot be killed physically, because I cannot be killed, neither can he. Our souls and lives are mixed and in the hands of God and God alone. Does that clear it up" Bizerc asked?

SHANE

The big red demon walked to the next bed and bitch slapped Wolf's lifeless body so hard that the bed snapped.

"Get your ass up, we have work to do" Bizerc yelled in anger or Wolf.

The man's eyes opened and they were orange and he began to change. Where once there was Wolf, now there was the biggest werewolf alive. All of the other wolves took a knee and bowed their head to the Alpha wolf in respect.

"You knew" Jazon said to Ajay. It was not a question.

"Yes, he made me swear not to tell for your safety Jazon" Ajay answered in anger.

Jazon looked at his friend and brother in everything but blood and smiled.

"It is okay Ajay, you always got my back, I trust your judgment" Jazon said.

Terry was vibrating literally; he could not contain what he had to say much longer. He finally had enough wasting time and stomped his foot hard.

"Listen to me, and keep all your mouths shut until I finish" Terry said in a serious tone that brooked no argument.

"Speak son" Wolf said.

"I went out and searched the wooded area and I caught a scent so I followed it, guess where it went? Finney's old office and then from there to the airport; I was unsure what to do until I was handed a note with your name on it" Terry said.

"Well give me my note" Jazon said.

"It is not you name on the envelope Jazon, it is his" Terry said pointing at Ajay.

Ajay was holding Silky in his arms and his eyes were on her lovely slumbering face. He did not even look up at the mention of clues to the assassins; he was lost in his own private hell at the moment.

"Ajay" Jazon said placing a hand on his friend shoulder.

Ajay looked up, he was lost in grief, he reached out and took the letter out of Terry's hand. Ajay opened the envelope and unfolded the paper and began to read.

In the other side of the room Father Mick Sully was chatting with Bizerc and then he asked if he could touch his wings? The fire Demon was amused and told the Pastor he could but the Demon warned him that he was hot to the touch not just warm. Mick ran his hand over Bizerc's wing and it burnt his hand a bit, but that did not stop the Pastor from continueing.

"So do you have evil in you Bizerc, or are you filled with fire; like you seem to be" Mick asked?

"I am filled with love for the boy, and the spirit of the lord. I am a fallen angel Mick, I repented my sins and stupidity and begged to make it up to the LORD, I am granted a conditional pardon, and the boy is the condition. I am happy to be of service to my God again. Biz is a good host and friend, he does not speak out loud but his mind can talk into other's minds whenever he wishes and we talk non-stop to each other" Bizerc explained.

The room erupted in to a string out profanity that I am inclined not to repeat. Ajay put Silky down softly and stomped over to Jazon and slammed the letter into his chest looked him in the eyes and then left the room, for his own room and his weapons. Jazon opened the letter and read it. He handed the paper to Pegi who read it out loud for the rest of the room.

(Hello Ajay, yes I have learned your name. You have helped that no good son of a bitch Jazon Wild to ruin me, you have hunted and killed my brethren and stolen my servants. So, I have decided to return the favor, I have burned your home, killed your friends and poisoned your lover. She will live only if you come to me and offer me you neck; so that I can taste your blood. If you do that Ajay Rey, I will give you the cure for your lover's illness, until then she will die slowly over the next six months. Any time passed then is too late and she will die for sure. I am looking forward to seeing you again.

Sincerely:

Brian J. Finney

PS: leave you dog and Jazon behind, come alone.)

Pegi finished and looked around the room, Jazon was gone; no doubt to follow Ajay. Terry looked at Wolf. The leader nodded his head and Terry was a blur even in human form leaving.

"What just happened" Jax asked?

It was Bizerc who answered for the group.

"Jax, they are going to hunt down the guilty and slay them. Terry just asked silently for permission to guard Ajay's back, even though Jazon will be there to do that; Terry would not let them go alone" Bizerc explained.

"I am going as well, it is my fault that they got into our home and nearly burned it down. If I had stopped them here; they would never have gotten to you at the club. I have a debt that I have sworn to pay back, I will not break my word" Jc said in a rough voice.

(IN THE ARMORY)

Jazon found Ajay in his room getting a bag packed, Jazon whistled and said one word before he left to pack his own bags.

SHANE

"Armory" Jazon said.

"Be right there brother" Ajay said without looking up.

In the armory, Jazon took Ajay to the back where only Jazon and Tad ever went. Jazon pulled out a key and put it into a lock and the cabinet did not open; the entire wall did. Ajay smiled even though he was deeply angry at the moment. Jazon pulled him through the wall as it closed.

"This is Tad's private armory and workshop. I had him make you this metal fiber-mesh garment. It with cover your feet all the way up to your ears. It will stop anything short of a laser from penetrating it. It also has a hood and goggles so you are totally protected. I want you to wear it under your clothes always. You can was it in the shower, shake it and put it back on, it is quite incredible" Jazon said.

Ajay stripped down and put on the under clothing sheer body armor. He tucked the hood into his bag and was about to leave when Jazon said to hold up. Jazon opened a case and it was full of what looked like silver pencils. They were in fact mini hollow crossbow arrows filled with holy water and garlic. Jazon showed Ajay how to load five darts into the mini folding bow. When Ajay got it down, Jazon put the case in Ajay's bag, along with some nasty looking blades. Lastly, Jazon took a cross with a blood red gem from the jeweler's case and gave it to Ajay, who put it around his neck.

"The gem is my blood crystallized, if your going to die remove the gem and swallow it, it might save your life" Jazon said in a sad voice.

Jazon took his assassin's sword and two sword swords off the wall where Tad kept them and followed Ajay out the door and up the stair. Terry was waiting for them at the top next to Jc who had a long bag and his skateboard.

"I am not for long goodbyes, we love you guys and we will try to return as soon as we can. If we don't, Wolf make sure that this hotel lives and Ask Alister to shield you from the other clans, since his is by far the strongest one left" Jazon said.

Pegi cried but kissed all four boys and then left for the kitchen. The wolves shook the boy's hands, but no words were exchanged. Father Sully blessed all four and said his farewell. Lastly, Jax held Jazon so tight he could feel her heart pounding as if it were in his chest. Jazon refused to say goodbye to her, and she did not offer a goodbye either or tears.

Alister did not like the method Brian choose to revenge himself and thought him a coward, therefore he arrange a private Jet plane to Dublin, once there the boys were on their own.

Four warrior left their only home and loved ones and set off to rid the world of the enemy of humanity, and the magical community as well.

SHANE

EPILOG

In a castle in a small Irish township, the lord of all of Europe sits drinking wine with his vineyard master in the great hall of O'Day Keep. This is a regular tradition with every harvest and wine making. Collin O'Day who is a twelve hundred year old vampire, loves human food and wine. He is a good lord as well, he is not in the habit of letting his subject be eaten by rogue vampires or anything else. His Wine master knows what Collin is and loves the man anyway. His family has served the House of the O'Day clan for as long as they have existed and never has even one of his family been harmed. Amus Savage was a portly man with a happy face, he was in his forty fifth year of life. He was wealthy by most men's standard but his friendship with Collin was his prized possession. Collin felt the same way about Amus.

(GONG)

The door gong that Collin brought back from China when he visited his friend the Khan, whom ruled Asia like he did Europe, just bonged, so the servants went to announce whom ever came to call. There was a crashing noise and one of the servants came bouncing

SHANE

into Collin's view bleeding. Collin was very kind to his staff, and anyone who injured them just signed a death sentence. In a flash Collin burst to speed.

"Geet out of me wee, or I'll kill ya" A vampire screamed!

Collin had the black-heart by the throat when he let him go in disgust.

"I thought I banished you from my lands" Collin announced loudly.

"True but a new hunter came and burned Brian and me out in America; He seems to be determined to wipe out all vampires, from the top down. I came to warn you" Mark said.

Collin looked over Mark and was unpleased as usual. He could not understand how his blood could flow through this trash before him.

"I will grant you a short stay in my lands, until I can confirm or abolish the news you brought me. One more thing" Collin said as he back handed mark into a stone wall. "You will not touch my staff or any other human in Europe or I will cut your heart out personally. Do you understand me"?

"Yes sir, I will obey you" Mark said quickly.

Secretly Mark had hoped that Brian would challenge his Great grandfather to a duel and kill him, thus mark would become Lord O'day over Europe. However, Brian did not want to risk it, Collin was not to be trifled with; he killed every opponent he had ever had and was old and extremely powerful. Collin was soft toward Human, that would someday spell his doom, maybe that day had come. Mark had set in motion the wheels that would bring then Hunter Jazon here to Ireland. Collin would not allow a hunter on his lands, so they would be sure to kill each other, or at the least one would parish. Life was good mark thought.

SHANE

VAMPIRE HERO SAGA

SHANE

CHARACTERS OF THE NIGHT:

Jazon Wild: human/vampire, day light vampire light brown hair, brown red or blue eyes, 5'7, 148, super fast and strong, immune to sunshine, garlic, holy water, crosses, and is for God he unlikely servant, hero.

Ajay Rey: human, black fella, 5'10, 200lbs, pro ball player, Jazon's bff, vampire hunter

Jax Koft: human, female, Jazon's lover, bartender, 5'5 110lbs, short red-black hair green eyes, perfect body

Father Mick Sully: pastor, 55, 5'9 245, grey hair, human, Jazon and Ajays's support coordinator

Mark O'Day: Irish vampire, red hair, 5'4 140, dirt bag, killer coward, bit Jazon and turned him

Collin O'Day: Vampire master,1200 year old Jazon's great, great grand uncle, on his mother's side

Wolf Peters: Human/werewolf Jazon's ally and friend, golden brown hair 5'10 175lbs, 7' 400lbs in wolf form

Tad Orielly: gnome, 4ft, 150lbs, 600yrs old good guy

SHANE

Bryan Finney: Vampire, Jazon's enemy, 6', 185, blond, pale blue eyes, charming murderer, Prince of Portland

Silky: wood nymph, 5ft, 85 lbs, Ajay's on the side monster gf, green eyes , tan skin, brown hair, good side

Pegi; female human,(205yrs old) semi hillbilly, tough ol lady, funny, no bs type, not afraid of anything, helps Ajay support Jazon

Bizerc (Biz): Human hybrid, brown hair, green eyes (sometimes Red) quiet, mysterious, Wolf's friend and Jazon's ally

PAT Marks: Human, A local Butcher, Christian, helper of Jazon and father sully

Enoch: giant werewolf. Black man, black eyes, bald, deep voice, scarred up.

Gilly: old vampire, insane, blood eyes, shaved head. 6', 200lbs, uses many different blades to kill, hates guns. Used to be a sailor in the 1700's

TERRY: WEREWOLF, 15 years old, brown hair 6'3 220 as a human, 400lbs in wolf form. Smart mouth, trouble maker, good fighter.

Block: Troll 12ft 1000lbs,green brown skin, smells like apple pie for an unknown reason. strong ass a

bulldozer and immortal, cant be killed by anything know. He is a good guy, very polite and protective.

Jc: Werewolf shape shifter, 3 forms, pure wolf, werewolf and skate punk. Shady and fun

DEMI: the human girl Brian Finney held hostage over Jc, so that the werewolf would do his bidding, she died of starvation, she refused to be Jc's down fall

Alister the White; 560yr old vampire, blue eyes , white hair, handsome, kind of a human lover. He is the one vampire friend Jazon has. Very powerful and respected.

ORSON SWELLS: fat vampire lord over 1/3 of California, old, smart, cowardly.

Lars Mense: thin mouse faces vampire lord over 1/3 of California, old, mean, tricky

Robert Owens: vampire, 40-ish, funny, tough as nails, lords over 1/3 of California and the speaker for all three clans, i f it comes to it

Amus Savage: human wine and Vineyard master for Collin O'Day 45 yrs old

SHANE

OTHER BOOKS BY THIS AUTHOR:

DESTINY'S KEY: 2008

BREATH OF MAGIK: 2009

THE VAMPIRE WARS: Beginning 2009

ENTER THE GUARDIANS: KYL 2009

GUARDIANS- GROT: 2009

BLOOD BY DAY 2009 (vampire hero 1)

SHADOWS REVENGE 2009 (Vamp hero2)

SHADOW GUARD (VAMPIRE HERO 3)

BLACK WINGS: 2009 (Next LOL)

HOUSE OF THE WOLF: TBA

VAMPIRE WARS 2 TBA

WORLD OF ICE (KIDS NOVEL)

SHANE

ABOUT THE AUTHOR:

Shane was born Dec 21st, in Portland Oregon, to his mother Toffy Lee Wilson and Oscar Joel Wilson. He has an older sister Cookie Caroline Sinclair and a younger brother Curtis Casey Wilson.

Shane currently lives in Vancouver Washington with his Wife of over twenty years, Arlene; and he son Joston and his daughter Jessica Lee.

Shane races Quads and has won 12 over all championships. Joston has won two and Jessica has one title to her credit as well.

Shane has studied Martial arts for nearly thirty years and has a 5th degree black belt in KAJUKENBO.

Shane loves to entertain people with his stories; so her beautiful wife bought him a laptop and told him to put them all to paper. It is Shane's goal to write 100+ books and publish them all. At his current rate; he will reach his goal in under ten years time.

Shane offers this bit of advice:

"IF YOU THINK YOU CAN; THEN YOU ARE RIGHT. IF YOU THINK YOU CAN'T THEN YOU ARE ALSO RIGHT. THEREFORE, NEVER LET ANYTHING BEAT YOU!"

MY PERSON MANTRA IS:

I CAN'T BE BEAT; BECAUSE I WONT BE BEAT.

I MAY NOT ALWAYS WIN, BUT I NEVER LOOSE.

GOD BLESS YOU AND I LOVE YOU

BTW: STAY TUNED FOR BOOK 2 SHADOWS REVENGE

SHANE

www.ingramcontent.com/pod-product-compliance
Lightning Source LLC
Chambersburg PA
CBHW050515260626
47157CB00004B/1334